"There are paparazzi everywhere. Please get into the car."

It was only then that Emmeline realized that camera flashes were popping right and left. Not because of her—but because Sheikh Al-Koury was one of the world's most powerful men.

He smiled at her, firm lips quirking as if amused, and yet she knew he couldn't be, not when his silver gaze glittered like frost. "It wasn't a request. I'm not negotiating. Get in the car."

Clinging to the last shred of her dignity, she lifted her chin, moved past the paparazzi and stepped gracefully into the car, her turquoise satin dress swishing across the leather as she slid across the seat to the far side.

Emmeline sucked in a breath of silent protest as Makin settled next to her, far too close. She waited to give the name of her hotel until the driver had pulled from the curb. "I'm staying at The Breakers," she said, hands compulsively smoothing the creases marring the satin of her skirt. "You can drop me off there."

Sheikh Al-Koury didn't even glance at her. "I won't be dropping you anywhere. We're heading to the airport. I'll have the hotel pack up your things and send them to the airport to meet our plane."

For a moment she couldn't speak. "Plane?"

"We're going to Kadar."

A Royal Scandal

When blue blood runs hot…

Separated at birth, twin sisters Hannah and Emmeline had very different upbringings; Hannah was raised in a small town in Texas, while Emmeline took her rightful place as princess, enjoying a life of unequaled privilege.

Reunited years later, the identical sisters cause the scandal of the century by swapping places and posing as each other.

But now their paths have crossed with two powerful rulers—and their princess-and-pauper charade is about to be exposed.…

Last month you read Hannah's story in

NOT FIT FOR A KING?

This month read Princess Emmeline's story in

HIS MAJESTY'S MISTAKE

Jane Porter

HIS MAJESTY'S MISTAKE

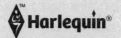
Harlequin®

TORONTO NEW YORK LONDON
AMSTERDAM PARIS SYDNEY HAMBURG
STOCKHOLM ATHENS TOKYO MILAN MADRID
PRAGUE WARSAW BUDAPEST AUCKLAND

Recycling programs
for this product may
not exist in your area.

ISBN-13: 978-0-373-13081-8

HIS MAJESTY'S MISTAKE

www.Harlequin.com

Printed in U.S.A.

All about the author…
Jane Porter

JANE PORTER grew up on a diet of Harlequin romances, reading late at night under the covers so her mother wouldn't see. She wrote her first book at age eight, and spent many of her high school and college years living abroad, immersing herself in other cultures and continuing to read voraciously. Now Jane splits her time between rugged Seattle, Washington, and the beautiful beaches of Hawaii, with her sexy surfer and three very active sons. Jane loves to hear from her readers. You can write to her at P.O. Box 524, Bellevue, WA 98009, U.S.A. Or visit her website at www.janeporter.com.

Other titles by Jane Porter available in eBook

Harlequin Presents®

CHAPTER ONE

ALEJANDRO had to be here.

Had to be.

Because if he wasn't at Mynt Lounge, South Beach's trendiest nightclub, he wasn't in South Beach any longer. She'd checked the other clubs first and she knew Alejandro. He only did cool. He only did chic. It was Mynt Lounge or nothing. And it had to be here because she had to see him.

Ignoring the dozens of young American women queuing outside in stiletto heels and skirts so short they barely covered their assets, Princess Emmeline d'Arcy of Brabant stepped from her cab onto the curb and tucked a long gleaming strand of hair behind her ear. She would make Alejandro listen to reason. She'd make him see her position and surely he'd change his mind once he understood what was at stake.

Her name.

Her reputation.

And even more importantly, the future and security of their child.

Her stomach rose in protest and she willed the nausea to pass. She wouldn't get sick here, not when everything was riding on the next five minutes.

Air bottled in her lungs, shoulders squared, Princess Emmeline d'Arcy of the European commonwealth Brabant headed straight for the entrance, bypassing the line that snaked around the building and down the side street.

Alejandro would honor the promise he'd made her. He'd be a man and keep his word. He had to.

As Emmeline approached the front door, the club bouncer dropped the red velvet rope for her, giving her instant admission into the exclusive club. He didn't know Emmeline personally. He had no idea she was a European royal. But it was clear to everyone present that she was someone important. A VIP. And Mynt Lounge was all about celebrities, models and VIPs. It had, reputedly, the tightest door policy in all of South Beach.

Inside the darkened club, giant stars and metallic balls hung from the ceiling as futuristic go-go girls danced on the bar in nonexistent costumes and white thigh-high boots. A wall of purple lights flashed behind the DJ and other lights shifted, painting the writhing crowd on the dance floor purple, white and gold, leaving corners shadowy.

The princess paused, her long black lashes dropping as she scanned the interior looking for Alejandro, praying he'd be here. Praying he hadn't left South Beach yet for tomorrow's polo tournament in Greenwich. His horses had already gone, but he usually followed later.

A cocktail waitress approached and Emmeline shook her head. She wasn't here to party. She was here to make sure Alejandro did the right thing. He'd made love to her. She'd gotten pregnant. He'd vowed to take care of her. And now he'd better do it.

She wanted a ring, a wedding date and legitimacy for their unborn child.

He owed that much to her.

It had never been her plan to leave Europe, but she'd learned to love Alejandro's Argentina. They could live outside Buenos Aires on his estancia and have babies and raise horses.

It was a different future than the one her family had planned for her. She was to have been Queen of Raguva, married to King Zale Patek, and her family would be upset. For one thing, Alejandro wasn't a member of the aristocracy, and for another, he had a bit of a reputation, but once they were married, surely her mother and father would accept him. Alejandro was wealthy. He could provide for them. And she believed in her heart that he would provide, once he understood she had nowhere to go, no other options. European princesses didn't become single mothers.

While she'd never wanted to marry King Zale Patek, she did respect him. She couldn't say the same for Alejandro, and she'd slept with him.

Stupid. Stupid to sleep with someone you didn't love, hoping that maybe he did love you, and would want you and protect you…rescue you…as if you were Rapunzel locked high in the ivory tower.

Emmeline shuddered, horrified. But what was done was done and now she had to be smart. Keep it together.

Swallowing convulsively, Emmeline smoothed the peacock-blue satin fabric of her cocktail dress over her hips. She could feel the jut of her hipbones beneath her trembling hands. She'd never been this thin before, but she couldn't keep anything down. She was sick morning, noon and night, but she prayed that once she hit the second trimester the nausea would subside.

From the VIP section in the back she heard a roar of masculine laughter. Alejandro. So he *was* here.

Her stomach fell, a wild tumble, even as her limbs stiffened, body tight, humming with anxiety.

He'd been ignoring her, avoiding her calls, but surely once he saw her, he'd remember how much he'd said he adored her. For five years he'd chased her, pursuing her relentlessly, pledging eternal love. She'd resisted his advances for years, too, but then in a weak moment earlier in the spring, she'd succumbed, giving him her virginity.

It hadn't been the passionate experience she'd hoped for. Alejandro had been impatient, even irritated. She'd been surprised by the emptiness and roughness of the lovemaking but told herself that it'd be better the next time, that as she grew to love him, she'd learn how to relax. She'd learn how to respond. She'd heard that sex was so different when you were emotionally close and she hoped that it was true.

But there hadn't been a next time. And now she was pregnant.

Ridiculous. Horrifying. Especially as she was engaged to another man. It was an arranged marriage, one that had been planned years ago for her when she was still in her teens, and the wedding was scheduled for just ten days from now. Obviously she couldn't marry King Patek pregnant with Alejandro's baby. So Alejandro needed to man up. Do the right thing, and accept his responsibility in this catastrophe.

Shoulders thrown back, head high, Emmeline entered the darkened VIP room, her narrowed gaze scanning the low plush couches filled with lounging guests. She spotted Alejandro right away. He was hard to miss in his billowy white shirt that showed off his dark hair, tan skin and handsome Latin profile to perfection. He wasn't alone. He had a stunning young brunette in a shocking red mini-dress on his lap.

Penelope Luca, Emmeline thought, recognizing the young model who had recently become the new It girl. But Penelope wasn't merely sitting on Alejandro's lap. Alejandro's hand was up underneath the young model's short red skirt, his lips were nuzzling her neck.

For a moment Emmeline couldn't move or breathe. For a moment she stood transfixed by the sight of Alejandro pleasuring Penelope.

And then humiliation screamed through her.

This was the man who'd promised to love her forever? This was the man who wanted her, Emmeline d'Arcy, above all others? This was the man she'd sacrificed her future for?

"Alejandro." Her voice was low, clear and sharp. It cut through the pounding music, hum of voices and shrill laughter. Heads turned toward Emmeline. She was dimly aware that everyone was looking at her but she only had eyes for Alejandro.

He looked up at her from beneath his lashes, his lips still affixed to the girl's neck, his expression mocking.

He didn't care.

Emmeline's legs shook. The room seemed to spin.

He didn't care, she thought again, horror mounting. He didn't care if she saw him with Penelope. He didn't care how Emmeline felt. Because he didn't care for her. He'd never cared, either.

It hit her that it had all been a game for him…to bed a princess. The challenge. The chase. The conquest. She'd merely been a beautiful royal scalp to decorate his belt. And now that he'd possessed her, taken her innocence, he'd discarded her. As if she were nothing. No one.

Fury and pain blinded her. Fury with herself, pain for her child. She'd been stupid, so stupid, and she had no one to blame but herself. But wasn't that her problem? Hadn't that been her Achilles' heel her entire life? Needing love? Craving validation?

Her weakness sickened her, shamed her. Nausea hit her in waves.

"Alejandro," she repeated his name, her voice dropping, breaking, fire licking her limbs, daggers slicing her heart. "I will not be ignored!"

But he did ignore her. He didn't even bother to look at her again.

Her legs shook. Her eyes burned. How dare he mock her this way. She marched closer, temper blazing. "You're a liar and a cheat. A pathetic excuse for a man—"

"Stop." A deep, hard male voice spoke from behind her, interrupting her, even as a hand settled on her shoulder.

She struggled to shake the hand off, not finished with Alejandro yet. "You will take responsibility," she insisted, trembling with rage.

"I said, enough," Sheikh Makin Al-Koury repeated tersely, head dropped, mouth close to Hannah's ear. He was angry, very angry, and he told himself it was because his assistant had gone missing in action, and that he resented having to chase her down like a recalcitrant puppy, but it was more than that.

It was her, Hannah, dressed like…looking like…sex. Sex in high heels.

Impossible. Hannah wasn't sexy. Hannah wasn't hot, but here she was in a cocktail dress so snug that it looked painted on her slim body, the turquoise satin fabric clinging to her small, firm breasts and outlining her high, round ass.

The fact that he noticed her ass blew his mind. He'd never even looked at her body before, didn't even know she had a body, and yet here she was in a tight shimmering dress with kohl-rimmed eyes, her long dark hair tumbling free over her shoulders.

The thick tousled hair cascading down her back drew his eye again to her ass, and desire flared, his body hardening instantly.

Makin gritted his teeth, disgusted that he was responding to his assistant like an immature schoolboy. For God's sake. She'd worked for him for nearly five years. What was wrong with him?

She tried to jerk away from him, and his palm slid across the warm satin of her bare shoulder. She felt as hot and erotic as she looked, and he hardened all over again, her smooth soft skin heating his.

Stunned that she was being manhandled, Emmeline d'Arcy turned her head sharply to get a look behind her but all she could see was shoulders—endless shoulders—above a very broad chest covered in an elegant charcoal dress shirt.

"Unhand me," she choked, angling her head back to get a better look at him, but she couldn't see his face, not without turning all the way around. Her vision was limited to his chin and jaw. And it wasn't an easy jaw. He was all hard lines—strong, angular jaw, square chin, the fierce set of firm lips. The only hint of softness she could see was the glimpse of dark bronze skin at his throat where his collar was open.

"You're making a fool of yourself," he said harshly, his English lightly accented, his voice strangely familiar.

But why was his voice familiar? Did she know him? More importantly, did he know her? Was he one of her father's men? Had her father, King William, sent someone from his security, or King Patek?

She craned her head to get a better look, but he was so tall, and the club so very dark. "Let me go," she repeated, unwilling to be managed by even her father's men.

"Once we're outside," he answered, applying pressure to her shoulder.

She shuddered at the warmth of his skin against hers.

"I'm not going anywhere. Not until I've spoken with Mr. Ibanez—"

"This is neither the time or place," he said, cutting her short. His hand moved from her shoulder to her wrist, his fingers clamping vise-like around her fragile bones.

He had a tight grip, and she shivered as heat spread through her. "Release me," she demanded, tugging at her wrist. *"Immediately."*

"Not a chance, Hannah," he answered calmly, and yet his tone was so hard and determined that it rumbled through her, penetrating deep to rattle her bones.

Hannah.

He thought she was Hannah.

Her heart faltered. A cold shivery sensation slid down her spine as she put the pieces together. His deep, familiar voice. His extraordinary height. His ridiculous strength.

Sheikh Makin Al-Koury, Hannah's boss. Emmeline stiffened, realizing she was in trouble—she'd spent the past four days impersonating his personal assistant.

And then he was dragging her from the club, through the crowded dance floor and out the front door.

Emmeline's head spun as they stepped outside, away from the blinding lights and gyrating bodies on the bar and dance floor. The heavy nightclub door swung closed behind them, silencing the thumping music.

It was only then that he released her and turning, she looked straight up into Sheikh Al-Koury's face. He wasn't happy. No, make that he was livid.

"Hello," she said, voice cracking.

One of his strong black eyebrows lifted. "Hello?" he repeated incredulously. "Is that all you have to say?"

She licked her lips but her mouth remained too dry and her lips caught on her teeth.

Five days ago it had seemed like a brilliant idea to beg Hannah, the American who looked so much like her, to change places with her for a few hours so Emmeline could escape her security detail at the hotel and confront Alejandro. Hannah had become a blonde and Emmeline a brunette. They'd changed hairstyles, wardrobes and lifestyles. It was to have been for a few hours, but that had been days ago and since then everything had become so very complicated as Hannah was now in Raguva, on the Dalmatian Coast, masquerading as Princess Emmeline, while Emmeline was still here in Florida, pretending to be Hannah.

"Wh-what are you doing here?" she stuttered now, staring up into Sheikh Makin Al-Koury's face, trapped in his light eyes. His eyes were gray, the lightest gray, almost silver, and his expression so fierce her legs went weak.

"Saving you from making a complete ass of yourself," he answered grimly. He had a face that was too hard to be considered classically handsome—square jaw, strong chin, high slash of cheekbones, with a long straight nose. "Have you completely lost your mind?"

Desperation sharpened her voice. "I have to go back in. I must speak with him—"

"He didn't seem interested," Sheikh Al-Koury interrupted as if bored.

Heat rushed through her, heat and shame, because Sheikh Al-Koury was right. Alejandro hadn't been the least bit interested, not with the stunning Penelope on his lap, but that didn't change her goal. It just meant she had to work harder to make Alejandro see reason. "You don't even know who I'm talking about."

"Alejandro Ibanez," he retorted. "Now get into the car—"

"I can't!"

"You must."

"You don't understand." Panic filled her, tears burning her eyes. She could not, would not, be a single mother. She'd be cut off from her family. She'd be out on the streets. And yes, she'd been named an honorary chair for a dozen different charities, but in reality, she had no skills to speak of. If Alejandro didn't help them, how would she and the child survive? "I must speak with him. It's urgent."

"That may be, but there are paparazzi everywhere and your Mr. Ibanez appeared…unavailable…for a proper discussion. Please get into the car."

It was only then that Emmeline realized that camera flashes

were popping right and left. Not because of her—the media thought she was ordinary Hannah Smith—but because Sheikh Al-Koury was one of the world's most powerful men. His country, Kadar, produced more oil than any other country or kingdom in the Middle East. Western powers tripped over themselves to befriend him. And Emmeline's lookalike, Hannah Smith, had been his assistant for years.

"I'll take a cab back to my hotel," she said huskily, nausea washing through her in waves.

Sheikh Al-Koury smiled at her, firm lips quirking as if amused, and yet she knew he couldn't be, not when his silver gaze glittered like frost. "I'm afraid you misunderstood me." He paused, his gaze lingering on her face. "It wasn't a request, Hannah. I'm not negotiating. Get in the car."

For a moment she couldn't breathe, feeling smashed, squashed. He was smiling, though, but that was because he intended to win. Powerful men always did.

Clinging to the last shred of her dignity, she lifted her chin, moved past the paparazzi, and stepped gracefully into the car, her turquoise satin dress swishing across the leather as she slid across the seat to the far side.

Emmeline sucked in a breath of silent protest as Makin settled next to her, far too close. She crossed one leg over the other, trying to make herself smaller. He was too big and physical. He exuded energy, intensity and it made her heart race so fast she felt dizzy.

Emmeline waited until the driver had pulled from the curb to give the name of her hotel. "I'm staying at the Breakers," she said, hands compulsively smoothing the creases marring the satin of her skirt. "You can drop me off there."

Sheikh Al-Koury didn't even glance at her. "I won't be dropping you anywhere. We're heading to the airport. I'll have the hotel pack up your things and send them to the airport to meet our plane."

For a moment she couldn't speak. "Plane?"

"We're going to Kadar."

Her pulse quickened yet again, her hands curling into fists. She wouldn't panic. Not yet. "Kadar?"

His gaze met hers and held. "Yes, Kadar, my country, my home. I'm hosting a huge conference in Kasbah Raha in a few days. Two dozen dignitaries are attending with their spouses. That was your idea. Remember?"

Emmeline pressed the fists down against her thighs. She knew nothing about organizing conferences or hosting international polo tournaments or any of the other dozen things Hannah did as Sheikh Al-Koury's assistant, but she couldn't admit that, not when Hannah was in Raguva pretending to be her. And if Texas-born Hannah could masquerade as a European princess, surely Emmeline could pass herself off as a secretary? How hard could it be?

"Of course," she answered firmly, feigning a confidence she did not feel. "Why wouldn't I?"

Again a strong black eyebrow lifted, his hard, harsh features hawk-like in the darkened limousine. "Because you've called in sick to work four days straight even as you've been spotted living it up all over town."

"I've hardly been living it up. I can't keep anything down, and I've only left my hotel room when absolutely necessary."

"Like tonight?"

"Yes."

"Because you had to see Mr. Ibanez."

Just hearing Alejandro's name sent a shock wave through her, because Alejandro hadn't just rejected her, he'd rejected the baby, too. She exhaled in a rush, devastated. "Yes."

"Why?"

Nausea rushed through her. "That's personal."

CHAPTER TWO

PERSONAL, Makin Al-Koury, His Royal Highness, Prince of Kadar, silently repeated, staring at Hannah from beneath his lashes, stunned that his sensible secretary had fallen for a man who had a woman in every city, as well as a wife and five children back at home.

"So what did he tell you?" Makin said coolly. "That he loved you? That he couldn't live without you? What did he say to get you into bed?"

Her porcelain cheeks turned pink and she pushed the heavy weight of her rich brown hair off her pale shoulder. "That's none of your business."

So Alejandro Ibanez had seduced her.

Makin bit down, his jaws clamped tightly together. He loathed very few people but Ibanez was at the top of the list. Moving in similar polo circles, Makin had witnessed Ibanez in action and the Argentine's tactic for getting women to sleep with him was simple—he seduced them emotionally and then bedded them swiftly. He'd convince a woman that she was special—unique—and that he couldn't imagine living without her. And women fell for it. Hook, line and sinker.

And apparently, Hannah had, too.

He'd known all week that something was wrong with Hannah. His secretary was practical and punctual, organized and calm. She didn't call in sick. She didn't show up late. She didn't make excuses. She was professional. Dedicated. Disciplined. The woman across the seat from him was none of the above.

For the past four days he'd tried to understand what had happened to his efficient secretary.

He'd pursued her as she pursued Alejandro Ibanez, and it wasn't until tonight, when he saw her in the club, that he understood.

She'd fallen in love with Alejandro and the Argentine had callously, carelessly used her before tossing her away, breaking her heart just as he'd broken that of every other woman who came his way.

Makin's chest felt tight and hot, and yet he wasn't a sensitive man, nor was he emotionally close to his employees. He was their boss. They worked for him. He expected them to do their job. End of story.

"Your personal life is impacting your professional life, which is impacting mine," he answered, offering her a small pleasant smile even though he felt far from pleasant on the inside.

Her lips compressed even as her eyes flashed at him. "I'm not allowed to be sick?"

"Not if you aren't truly sick," he said flatly. "In that case, you'd be taking personal days, not sick leave."

Although pale, she sat tall, chin tilted, channeling an elegance, even an arrogance, he'd never seen in her before. "I wasn't well," she said imperiously, her back so tall and straight she appeared almost regal. "I'm still not well. But you can think what you want."

His eyebrow lifted a fraction at her attitude, even as something in him responded to the challenge. Hannah had never spoken to him like this before and he grew warm, overly warm. His trousers suddenly felt too tight, and his gaze dropped to her legs. They were endless. Slim, long, bare, crossed high at her knee—

He stopped himself short. He was not going to go there. This was *Hannah*.

"I don't appreciate the attitude," he ground out. "If you'd like to keep your job, I'd drop it now."

She had the grace to blush. "I'm not giving you attitude. I'm merely defending myself." She paused, considered him from beneath her extravagant black lashes. "Or am I not allowed to do that?"

"There you go again."

"What?"

"Insolent, brash, defiant—"

"I'm confused. Am I an employee or a slave?"

For a moment he was silent, stunned by her audacity. What had happened to his perfect secretary? "Excuse me?" he finally said, his tone so deep and furious that she should have been silenced, but tonight Hannah seemed oblivious to any rebuke.

"Sheikh Al-Koury, certainly I'm allowed to have a voice."

"A voice, yes, provided it's not impudent."

"Impudent?" Her laugh was brittle. "I'm not a disobedient child. I'm twenty-five and—"

"Completely out of line." He leaned toward her, but she didn't shrink back. Instead she lifted her chin, staring boldly into his eyes. He felt another raw rush of emotion, his temper battling with something else…curiosity…desire…none of which, of course, was acceptable.

But there it was. This was a new Hannah and she was turning everything inside-out, including him.

And he didn't like it. Not a bit.

"You disappoint me," he said brusquely. "I expected more from you."

She tensed, pale jaw tightening, emotion flickering over her face, shadowing her eyes.

For a moment she looked fierce and proud and rather bruised.

A fighter without arms.

A warrior taken captive.

Joan of Arc at the stake.

He felt the strangest knotting in his chest. It was an emotion he hadn't felt before, and it was hot, sharp, uncomfortable. He didn't like it. He didn't want to feel it. She worked for him, not the other way around. "I don't know what game you're playing, but it's over. I've chased you from Palm Beach to South Beach but I'm not chasing anymore. Nor am I negotiating. It's my way, Hannah, or this is where it ends, and you can begin looking for a new job tomorrow."

He saw her chest rise and fall as she took a swift breath, but she didn't speak. Instead she held the air bottled in her lungs as she stared at him, a defiant light burning in her intensely blue eyes.

How could he have ever thought Hannah so calm and controlled? Because there was nothing calm or controlled about her now. No, nothing calm in those mysterious lavender-blue eyes at all. She was all emotion, hot, brilliant emotion that crackled in her and through her as though she were made of electricity itself.

Who was this woman? Did he even know her?

He frowned, his brow furrowing with frustration as his gaze swept over her from head to toe. At work she was always so buttoned-up around him, so perfectly proper, but then, she hadn't dressed for him tonight, she'd dressed for Alejandro, her lover.

The thought of her with Ibanez made his chest tighten again, as something in him cracked, shifted free, escaping from his infamous control to spread through him, hot, hard, possessive. For reasons he didn't fully comprehend, he couldn't stand the idea of Ibanez with her, touching her.

She was too good for Ibanez. She deserved so much better.

His gaze rested on her, and it was impossible to look away. Her satin dress was a perfect foil for her creamy skin and the rich chestnut hair that tumbled down her back. The low square neckline accentuated her long neck and exquisite features. He'd known that Hannah was attractive, but he'd never realized she was beautiful.

Incandescent.

Which didn't make sense. None of this really made sense because Hannah wasn't the sort of woman to glow. She was solidly stable, grounded, focused on work to the exclusion of all else. She rarely wore makeup and knew nothing about fashion, and yet tonight she appeared so delicate and luminous that he was tempted to brush his fingertips across her cheek to see what she wore to make her appear radiant.

The tip of her tongue appeared to wet her soft, full lower lip. His groin hardened as her pink tongue slid across and then touched the bow-shaped upper lip. For a moment he envied the lip and then he suppressed that carnal thought, too, but his body had a mind of its own and blood rushed to his shaft, heating and hardening him, making him throb.

"You're threatening to fire me, Sheikh Al-Koury?" Her incredulous tone provoked him almost as much as that provocative tongue slipping across her lips.

"You should know by now I never threaten, nor do I engage my employees in meaningless conversation. If I'm speaking to you it's because I'm conveying something important, something you need to know." He was hanging on to his temper by a thread. "And you should know that I've reached the end of my patience with you—"

"Not to be rude, Sheikh Al-Koury," she interrupted, before making a soft groaning sound. "But how far away is the airport? I think I'm going to be sick."

For Emmeline, the rest of the short drive to the executive airport passed in a blur of motion and misery. She remembered little but the limo pulling between large gates and then onto empty tarmac next to an impressively long white jet.

She was rushed up the stairs, aided by a flight attendant, and then escorted into a bedroom and through a door to a small bathroom.

The flight attendant flipped on the bathroom lights and then closed the door behind her, leaving Emmeline alone.

Thank God for small mercies.

Perspiration beading her brow, Emmeline crouched before the toilet. Her hands trembled on the pristine white porcelain as she leaned forward, her stomach emptying violently into the toilet bowl.

The acid that burned her throat was nothing compared to the acid eating away at her heart. This was all her fault…she had no one else to blame. She'd been weak and foolish and insecure. She'd reached out to the wrong man in a moment of need, and to make matters worse, she'd approached Hannah, dragging her into this.

Remorse filled her. Remorse and regret. Why wasn't she stronger? Why was she so needy? But then, when hadn't she craved love?

Gritting her teeth, she knew she couldn't blame her parents. They'd done their best. They'd tried. The fault was clearly hers. Apparently even at an early age she'd been clingy, always wanting to be held, needing constant reassurance and affection. Even as a little girl she'd been ashamed that she'd needed so much more than her parents could give.

Good princesses didn't have needs.

Good princesses didn't cause trouble.

Emmeline did both.

Emmeline's stomach churned and heaved all over again, and she lurched over the toilet, sick once more.

Tears stung her eyes. How could anyone call this morning sickness when she was ill morning, noon and night? She flushed the toilet again.

A quiet knocked sounded on the door. "Hannah?"

It was Makin Al-Koury. Emmeline's stomach performed a wild free fall which didn't help her nausea in the slightest. "Yes?"

"May I come in?"

No. But she couldn't say it. She was supposed to work for him. That meant she answered to him. Emmeline's eyes stung. "Yes."

The door softly opened and a shadow fell across the floor.

Blinking back tears, Emmeline glanced up as Makin filled the doorway. Tall and broad-shouldered, his expression was grim. There was no sympathy in his light gray eyes, no gentleness in the set of his jaw or the press of his firm mouth. But then, there'd been no gentleness earlier when he'd yanked her through the nightclub, pulling her onto the street, his hand gripped tightly around her wrist.

Even now, with her knees pressed to the cold tiled floor, she could feel the unyielding grip of his hand on her wrist, the heat of his skin against hers.

He'd been furious as his limousine traveled from the nightclub to the airport, and from his expression as he towered above her, he still was.

"Can I get you something?" he asked, his deep voice a raw rasp of sound in the small space.

She shook her head. "No. Thank you."

"You are sick."

She nodded, fighting fresh tears. "Yes."

"Why didn't you tell me?"

Her brow creased, eyebrows knitting. "I did."

His jaw tightened. He looked away, across the small bath, his lips flattening, making him look even more displeased. "Have you seen a doctor?"

"No."

"Why not? You said you can't keep anything down. You should have tests run, or see if the doctor could prescribe something that would help."

"It won't help—"

"Why not?"

She winced at the impatience and roughness in his voice. For a moment his mask slipped and she glimpsed something almost savage in his expression. "Because…"

Her voice faded as she got lost in his light eyes, and it crossed her mind that he might be the world's richest sheikh, but he wasn't entirely modern. Beneath his elegant, tailored suit and polished veneer was a man of the desert.

Because Sheikh Al-Koury wouldn't employ a pregnant, unwed woman, not even if she were American. It was a cultural issue, a matter of honor and respect. Emmeline might not be able to type quickly or place conference calls or create spreadsheets, but she'd spent enough time in the United Arab Emirates and Morocco to be familiar with the concept of *hshuma,* or shame. And an unwed pregnant woman would bring shame on all close to her, including her employer.

"It's just stress," she said. "I'm just…overly upset. But I'll pull myself together. I promise."

He looked at her so long and hard that the fine hair on Emmeline's nape lifted and her belly flip-flopped with nerves. "Then pull yourself together. I'm counting on you. And if you can't do your job anymore, tell me now so I can find someone who can."

"But I can."

He said nothing for several moments, his gaze resting on her face. "Why Ibanez?" he asked at last. "Why him of all people?"

She hunched her shoulders. "He said he loved me."

His jaw hardened, mouth compressing, expression incredulous. "And you believed him?"

She hesitated. "Yes."

Sheikh Al-Koury choked back a rough growl of protest. "I can't believe you fell for his lines. He says those lines to everyone. But you're not everyone. You're smart. You're educated. You should know better."

"I didn't."

"Couldn't you detect a false note in his flattery? Couldn't you see he's fake? That his lines were too slick, that he's as insincere as they come?"

"No." She drew a swift breath, making a hiccup of sound. "But I wish I had."

Makin battled his temper as he stared down at Hannah where she knelt on the floor, her shoulders sagging, her long chestnut hair a thick tangle down her thin back.

Someone else, someone soft, might be moved by her fragile beauty, but he refused to allow himself to feel anything for her, not now, not after she'd become a temptress. A seductress. A problem.

He didn't allow his personal and professional life to overlap. Sex, desire, lust…they didn't belong in the workplace. Ever.

"I respected you." His deep voice sounded harsh even to his own ears, but he'd never minced words with her before and wasn't about to start now. "And I'm not sure I do anymore."

She flinched, visibly stung, and his gut tightened, an uncomfortable cramp of sensation, and then it was gone, pushed away with the same ferocious intensity he'd applied to the rest of life.

He didn't cater to anyone—male or female. It went against his belief system. Makin had been his parents' only child and they'd been a very close, tight-knit family. His father, a powerful Bedouin ruler and Kadar's royal prince, was nearly twenty years older than Makin's French mother, Yvette.

When he was growing up, his parents had rarely discussed the past, being too focused on the present, but Makin had pieced enough details together to get a picture of his parents' courtship. They'd met when his mother was just twenty and a film student in Paris. She was beautiful and bright and full of big plans, but within weeks of meeting Tahnoon Al-Koury, she'd accepted his marriage proposal and exchanged her dreams for his, marrying him in a quiet ceremony in Paris before returning to Kadar with her new husband.

Makin had only met his maternal grandparents once, and that was at his father's funeral. His mother refused to speak to them so it'd been left to Makin to introduce himself to his French grandparents. They weren't the terrible people he'd imagined, just ignorant. They couldn't understand that their daughter could love an Arab, much less an Arab confined to a wheelchair.

Makin had grown up with his father in a wheelchair and it was neither terrible nor tragic, at least not until the end. His father was beyond brilliant. Tahnoon was devoted to his family, worshipped his wife and battled to maintain as much independence as he could, despite the degenerative nature of his disease.

Makin was twenty when his father died. But in the years Makin had with him, he never heard his father complain or make excuses, even though Tahnoon lived with tremendous pain and suffered endless indignities. No, his father was a proud, fierce man and he'd taught Makin—not by words, but by example— that life required strength, courage and hard work.

"You don't respect me because I wanted to be loved?" Hannah asked huskily, forcing his attention from the past to the present.

He glanced down, straight into her eyes, and felt that same uncomfortable twinge and steeled himself against the sensation. "I don't respect you wanting to be loved by *him*." He paused, wanting her to understand. "Ibanez is beneath you. He's self-centered and vulgar and the women who chase him are fools."

"That's harsh."

"But true. He's always at the heart of a scandal. He prefers married women or women recently engaged like that ridiculous Princess Emmeline—"

"Ridiculous Princess Emmeline?" she interrupted. "Do you know her?"

"I know of her—"

"So you can't say she's ridiculous—"

"Oh, I can. I know her family well, and I attended her sixteenth birthday in Brabant years ago. She's engaged to King Zale Patek, and I pity him. She's turned him into a joke by chasing after Ibanez all year despite her engagement to Patek. No one respects her. The princess has the morals of an alley cat."

"That's a horrid thing to say."

"I'm honest. Perhaps if others had been more honest with Her Royal Highness, she might have turned out differently." He shrugged dismissively. "But I don't care about her. I care about you and your ability to perform your job with clarity and efficiency. Don't let Ibanez waste another moment of your time. Nor my time, for that matter. Everything about him bores me." His gaze held hers. "Are we clear?"

"Yes," she said huskily.

"Then pull yourself together and take a seat in the main cabin so we can depart."

Using the vanity kit provided in the bathroom, Emmeline washed her face, brushed her teeth and ran a comb through her hair. The thick dark hair still looked strange to her. Emmeline missed her golden-blond color. Missed her wardrobe. Missed her life.

This is how Hannah must have felt when thrust into Emmeline's life.

Lost. Confused. Angry. And Emmeline knew she was the one who'd put Hannah in that position. Changing places with Hannah had been Emmeline's idea. There was no benefit for Hannah. Nothing to be gained by masquerading as a princess. It was Emmeline who'd benefited. She'd been able to slip away from her attendants to seek out Alejandro and tell him about the pregnancy. Only in the end, when she had confronted him, it hadn't mattered. He'd still rejected her.

Emmeline sucked in a slow breath, sickeningly aware that her selfishness and foolishness had impacted so many people. Hannah. King Patek. Sheikh Al-Koury.

What she had to do was fix things. Not just for her, but for everyone.

Once tidy and outwardly calm, she took the seat the flight attendant led her to, a seat not far from Makin's, although he was at work typing away on his laptop.

Emmeline tried to block him from her peripheral vision as the jet taxied down the runway, unnerved by the sheer size and shape of him.

He was tall, solid, muscular. As he typed, his arms flexed and she could see the distinct shape of his thick bicep press against the taut cotton of his shirt. His fine wool trousers silhouetted the hard cut of his quadriceps. Even his hands were strong, his fingers moving easily, confidently, across the laptop keyboard.

She watched his hands for a moment, fascinated by them. His skin was tan and his fingers were long and well-shaped. They reminded her of the hands on Greek statues—beautiful, classic, sculptural. She wondered what his touch would be like, and how his hands would move on a woman's body. Would his touch be light and gentle, or heavy and rough? She wondered how he held a woman, and if he curved her to him or held himself aloof, using her like a piece of equipment.

Emmeline had never wondered about such things before, but her night with Alejandro had changed all that. It changed the way she viewed men and women, made her realize that sex had been romanticized in books and movies and the media.

Sex wasn't warm or fun or intimate. It hadn't been beautiful or something pleasurable.

She'd found it a soulless, empty act. It'd been Alejandro taking her body—no more, no less than that.

Emmeline knew now her expectations had been so silly, so girlish and immature. Why hadn't she realized that Alejandro would pump away at her until he climaxed and roll off to shower and dress and leave?

Her eyes stung, hot, hot and gritty. Even seven weeks later she felt betrayed by her need for love and affection, and how she'd turned to Alejandro to give her that affection.

She'd imagined that sex would fill the hollow emptiness inside of her, but it had only made it worse.

Squeezing her eyes closed, she pulled the soft blanket even higher on her chest as her late grandmother's voice echoed in her head, "Don't cast pearls before swine." But that's what Emmeline had done out of desperation that no one would ever love her.

Emmeline shivered beneath the blanket, horrified all over again by her poor choices.

"Would you like me to turn the heat up?" Makin asked.

She opened her eyes and saw he was watching her. She didn't know how long he'd been watching. "I'm fine," she said unsteadily.

"I can get you another blanket."

"I'm fine," she repeated.

"You're shivering."

Heat crept into her cheeks. He was watching her closely, then. "Just my thoughts."

"Ibanez isn't worth your time. He's a liar, a cheat, a scoundrel. You deserve a prince of a man. Nothing less."

How ironic. Hannah deserved a prince of a man, but she, Emmeline, deserved only scorn.

Emmeline swallowed around the thick lump in her throat, wishing that she could be the smart, capable Hannah he admired instead of the useless spoiled princess he despised.

His disdain for her wounded. It shouldn't. He didn't know her, and she shouldn't let one person's opinion matter, but it did. He'd touched a nerve. A powerful nerve. It was as if he'd somehow seen through her elegant, polished exterior to the real Emmeline, the private Emmeline who felt so unworthy and impossible to love.

She'd always wondered why she felt so insecure, so alone, and then, on her sixteenth birthday, a half hour before her big party, she'd learned that her parents weren't her birth parents after all. She'd been adopted. Her birth mother had been a young unmarried woman from Brabant, but no one knew who her birth father was.

She'd gone to her birthday party absolutely shell-shocked. She didn't know why her adoptive father, King William, had felt compelled to break the news before her party but it had spoiled the night for her. Instead of dancing and celebrating with her guests, she'd found herself wondering about the mother who'd given her up, and if she looked like her, and if her mother ever thought of her.

It had been nine years since that revelation, and yet Emmeline still wondered about her birth parents. Could the fact that she'd been adopted have anything to do with her sense of emptiness and fear of abandonment? Could she have missed that mother who gave birth to her?

"What did you hope to accomplish tonight at the Mynt?" Makin suddenly asked.

She drew the blanket even closer to her chest, trying to capture more warmth. "He said he loved me—"

"Yes, I know," he interrupted impatiently. "You already told me that."

"—and I thought if he saw me tonight, he'd remember how he felt about me," she pressed on as though he hadn't spoken. "I thought he'd remember he'd asked me to marry him."

"He asked you to marry him?" he repeated, incredulous.

Her chin tilted defiantly. Why did he find that so impossible to believe? "Yes."

For a long moment Makin said nothing, absolutely nothing. He just sat there, looking at her as if he felt sorry for her. Just when Emmeline didn't think she could take his pitying silence another moment, he spoke. "Alejandro's already married. Not just married, but a father to five children. The oldest is twelve. The youngest just nine months old."

"Impossible."

"Have I ever lied to you about anything?"

She couldn't answer and, jaw flexing, he looked away, dropping his gaze to the bright screen of his laptop computer.

Blanket pressed to her collarbone, Emmeline's stomach heaved. Alejandro, already married? Father to five? Things just kept getting worse.

CHAPTER THREE

Hours later, Emmeline was woken by the vibration of the jet's landing gear unfolding, wheels in position in preparation for touching down. Half asleep, she glanced out the window but could see nothing below but pale gold...or was it beige? Maybe a little of both. No buildings, no lights, no roads, no sign of life. Just sand.

Emmeline groggily sat taller. Far in the distance she could see a spot of gray color. Or was it green? She didn't know what it was but it couldn't be a city, and there was no sprawling airport, either, and yet here they were making a sharp, steep descent as if they were about to land.

Just moments later, they touched down, the landing so smooth it was but a bump of sound and then the swift application of brakes. They hurtled along the black asphalt runway bordered on both sides by a vast reddish-gold desert. In the distance, in the same direction she'd spotted the gray-green patch, she could see a ragged range of mountains, but even those were copper and gold in the morning light.

She didn't know why, but she'd expected a city. Most of the royal princes she knew in Dubai and the UAE lived in cosmopolitan cities—glamorous centers filled with fashion boutiques and deluxe hotels and five-star restaurants. Sheikhs today were modern and wealthier than the rest of the world, including their European counterparts. They could afford life's every luxury, and they owned jets, yachts, rare cars, polo fields and strings of expensive ponies.

That was the world Emmeline had expected Sheikh Al-Koury to take her to. A sprawling urban city. But instead there was just sand. Sand and more sand. A virtual sea of sand in every direction, all the way to the rough-hewn mountains.

Emmeline had thought she could just put Hannah on a plane and get her here. But she wasn't going to be able to sneak Hannah into the desert and change places with her without anyone knowing. They were in such a deserted spot that all incoming aircraft would immediately be noticed.

"You look disappointed." Makin's deep voice came from across the aisle.

Emmeline's pulse quickened, and his deep husky timbre flooded her with memories—his appearance at the nightclub last night. His harsh opinion of Alejandro. His overwhelming physical presence.

"Why would I be disappointed?" she answered, with a casual arch of her eyebrow.

His silver gaze collided with hers and held. His features were granite-hard, his strong black eyebrows a slash above intense gray eyes. There was a light in his eyes, too, and a curve to his upper lip as if he weren't pleased with what he saw, either.

Her pulse jumped, racing wildly. He was still intense, still overwhelming, and nausea threatened to get the best of her.

"You've never liked the desert and Kasbah Raha," he said softly, his upper lip curling yet again. "You prefer life in Nadir with all the hustle and bustle."

So they truly were in the middle of nowhere. Which meant getting Hannah into Raha undetected would be as nearly impossible as Emmeline getting out.

"That may be so," she answered, hoping he didn't hear the wobble in her voice, "but I love how the morning sun burnishes the sand, turning everything copper and gold."

"How refreshing. You usually dread your time in the desert, saying Raha reminds you too much of your ranch in Texas."

Emmeline valiantly tried to play along. "But I love the ranch. It's where I grew up."

"Maybe. But in Nadir you have friends, your own apartment

in the palace, and numerous social activities, and when you're here, you're very much alone. Or alone with me."

The "alone with him" part sent a tremor of anxiety through her. She couldn't imagine spending another hour alone with him, much less days. She had to get Hannah here. Immediately.

His eyes suddenly gleamed, his full sensual mouth lifting in a mocking smile, and she could have sworn he knew exactly what she was thinking. She blushed, cheeks heating, skin prickling, even as she told herself it was impossible. He wasn't a mind reader. He couldn't possibly know how much he unsettled her.

And yet his gray eyes with those bright silver flecks were so direct, so perceptive she felt a quiver race through her, a quiver of dread and anticipation. He was so different from anyone she knew. So much more...

Makin's long legs stretched carelessly into the aisle and his broad shoulders filled his chair. He was at least six feet two. While Alejandro was handsome, Makin Al-Koury exuded power.

"Fortunately, this time here you'll be too busy assisting and entertaining my guests to feel isolated," he added. "I trust that everything's in place for their arrival?"

"Of course." She smiled to hide the fact that she didn't have a clue. But she'd soon find someone on his staff who would fill her in.

"Good. Because last night I seriously questioned your ability to pull this weekend off. But you slept most of the flight and appear more rested."

"I am," she answered, thinking that it was he who looked utterly fresh despite the fact that they'd been traveling for so long.

"Did you take something to help you sleep?"

"No. Why?"

"You aren't usually able to fall asleep on flights."

She didn't know how to respond to that as she'd learned to sleep on planes at a very young age. She'd grown up traveling. There were always royal functions and goodwill tours and appearances, first with her family and then on her own.

She'd been a shy little girl, and even a timid teenager, but the media never knew that. All they saw was her face and how photogenic she was. By the time she was fifteen, the paparazzi had singled her out, crowning her as the great beauty of her generation. Since then she'd lived in the spotlight, with camera lenses constantly focused on her and journalists' pens poised to praise or critique, and she never knew which until the article was published.

"I think I was too worn out not to sleep," she said, and it was true. All she wanted to do lately was sleep, and apparently that was another side effect of pregnancy. "And you? Did you get any rest?"

"Less than I wanted," he said, lashes dropping over his eyes, concealing his expression. "It was hard to sleep. I was—am—worried about you."

She heard something in his deep voice that made her insides flip-flop.

Genuine emotion. True concern.

He might hate Emmeline but he adored Hannah.

Emmeline felt a sharp stab of envy. What she wouldn't give to be the brilliant, efficient Hannah—a woman worthy of love and respect.

Awash in hot emotion, Emmeline looked away, out the jet's oval window. They'd finally come to a full stop in this vast desert. Uniformed personnel appeared on the tarmac. A fleet of shining black vehicles waited just off to the side of the runway, sunlight glinting off the windows and polished surfaces. Even though it was early, heat shimmered in iridescent waves off the black tarmac and surrounding sand.

This vast hot shimmering desert was Sheikh Al-Koury's world and now that she was here, Emmeline sensed her life would never be the same.

Makin stretched his legs out in the back seat of his custom car, a large, powerful sedan with tinted windows and reinforced panels to make it virtually bulletproof.

There hadn't been an uprising in Kadar in over three hundred years, and it was unlikely there would be in the next three hundred, but trouble could come from outside his country. The fact that he controlled so much oil had put a target on his back years ago. Fortunately, he wasn't a worrier, nor overly preoccupied with his own mortality. Instead he chose to live his life as his father had—without fear.

Makin relaxed a little, glad to be home.

His family had palaces all over Kadar but the rustic tribal kasbah in Raha had always been his favorite. Even the name Kasbah Raha—Palace of Rest—symbolized peace. Peace and calm. And it was. Here in the desert he was able to think clearly and focus without the noise and chaos of modern city life to distract him.

"Let's go over today's schedule," he said to Hannah, as his driver accelerated, leaving the tarmac and the sleek white jet behind. She was sitting to his left, pale but composed. He was glad to see her so calm. It gave him hope that all the personal drama was now behind them. "Which of my guests arrive first? And when?"

He waited for Hannah to reach for her briefcase or her phone but she did nothing. Had nothing. Instead she looked at him, her expression slightly baffled. "I don't…know."

He hesitated, thinking she was joking, not that she normally teased about things like that. But after a beat and a moment of awkward silence, he realized she was serious.

His jaw tightened, lips compressing as he understood that Hannah's personal problems were far from over.

Makin's frown deepened, eyebrows flattening above his eyes. "It's your job to know."

She took a quick breath. "It seems I've lost my calendar."

"But your calendar is backed up on your laptop. Where is your laptop computer?"

Her shoulders lifted and fell. "I don't know."

Makin had to turn away, look at something else other than Hannah. Her helplessness was getting to him. He didn't want to be angry with her, but he found everything about her provoking right now.

He focused on the desert beyond the car's tinted window, soothed by the familiar landscape. To someone else the desert might look monotonous with miles of red-gold sand in every direction, but he knew this desert like the back of his hand and it centered him now.

"You've lost your computer?" he asked finally, gaze fixed on the undulating dunes in the distance.

"Yes."

"How?"

"I think I must have left it somewhere when I wasn't…well."

"In South Beach?"

"Before that."

He turned his head sharply toward her. Her lavender-blue eyes appeared enormous in her pale face.

"It must have been Palm Beach," she added softly, fingers lacing together. "Just after the polo tournament. I had it for the tournament, but then it was gone."

"Why didn't you tell me sooner?"

"I should have. I'm sorry."

She looked so nervous and desperate that he bit back his criticism and took a deep breath instead. She'd just had her heart broken. She wasn't herself. Surely, he could try to be patient with her. At least for today.

He fought to keep his voice even. "Everything should be backed up on your desktop. When we get to the palace, you can go to your office and print off your calendar and update me later this afternoon."

"Thank you," she whispered.

He drew another breath as he considered her pale, tense face and rigid posture. Her shoulders were set, her spine elongated, her chin tilted. It was strange. Everything about her was strange. Hannah had never sat like this before. So tall and still, as if she'd become someone else. Someone frozen.

Which reminded him of last night on the airplane. His brow furrowed. "You talked in your sleep last night," he said. "Endlessly."

Her eyes met his and her lips parted but she made no sound.

"In French," he continued. "Your accent was impeccable. If I didn't know better, I'd think you were a native speaker."

"You're fluent in French?"

"Of course. My mother was French."

She flushed, her cheeks turning dark pink. "Did I say anything that would embarrass me?"

"Just that you are in terrible trouble." He waited, allowing his words to fall and settle before continuing. "What have you done, Hannah? What are you afraid of?"

A tiny pulse leapt at her throat and the pink in her cheeks faded just as quickly as it had bloomed there. "Nothing."

She answered quickly, too quickly, and they both knew it.

Makin suppressed his annoyance. Who did she think she was fooling? Didn't she realize he knew her? He knew her perhaps better than anyone. They'd worked so closely together over the years that he quite often knew what she would say before she said it. He knew her gestures and expressions and even her hesitation before she gave him her opinion.

But even then, they'd never been friends. Their relationship was strictly professional. He knew her work habits, not her life story. And he had to believe that if she'd gotten herself into trouble, she had the wherewithal to get herself out of it.

She was strong. Smart. Self-sufficient. She'd be fine.

Well, maybe in the long term, he amended. Right now Hannah looked far from fine.

She'd turned white, and he saw her swallow hard, once and again. She looked as if she was battling for control. "Do you need us to pull over?" he asked. "Are you—"

"Yes! Yes, please."

Makin spoke sharply to the driver and moments later they were parked on the side of the narrow road. She stumbled away from the car, her high heels sinking into the soft sand.

He wasn't sure if he should go after her—which is all he'd spent the last week doing—or give her some space to allow her to maintain some dignity.

Space won, and Makin and his driver stood next to the car in the event that their assistance was needed.

Even though it was still relatively early in the day, it was hot in the direct sun, with the morning temperature hovering just under a hundred degrees Fahrenheit. It was a very dry heat, he thought, sliding on his sunglasses, unlike Florida with its sweltering humidity.

Florida was fine, but this was his desert. This was where he belonged. They were just a few kilometers from Kasbah Raha now, and he was impatient to reach the palace.

He spent several months each year at Raha, and they were usually his favorite months.

Every day in Raha he'd wake, exercise, shower, have a light meal and then go to his office to work. He'd break for a late lunch and then work again, often late into the night. He enjoyed everything about his work and stayed at his desk because that's where he wanted to be.

He wasn't all work though. He had a mistress in Nadir whom he saw several times a week when there. Hannah knew about Madeline, of course, but it wasn't something he'd ever discuss with her. Just as Hannah had never discussed her love life with him.

Makin's cell phone suddenly rang, sounding too loud in the quiet desert. Withdrawing the phone from his trouser pocket, he saw it was his chief of security from the palace in Nadir.

Makin answered in Arabic.

As he listened, he went cold, thinking the timing couldn't be worse. Hannah was already struggling. This would devastate her.

Makin asked his chief of security to keep him informed and then hung up. As he pocketed his phone, Hannah appeared, her graceful hands smoothing her creased turquoise cocktail dress. As she walked toward him, she gave him an apologetic smile. "I'm sorry about that."

He didn't smile back. "You're still sick."

"Low blood sugar. Haven't eaten yet today."

Nor had anything to drink, he realized, remembering now that she'd no coffee, tea or juice on the flight, either.

Makin spoke to his driver in Arabic, and the chauffeur immediately went to the back of the gleaming car, opened the trunk, and withdrew two bottles of water. He gave both to the sheikh and Makin unscrewed the cap of one, and handed the open bottle to Hannah.

"It's cold," she said surprised, even as she took a long drink from the plastic bottle.

"I have a small refrigerator built into the trunk. Keeps things cool on long trips."

"That's smart. It's really hot here." She lifted the bottle to her lips, drank again, her hand trembling slightly.

Makin didn't miss the tremble of her hand. Or the purple shadows beneath her eyes. She was exhausted. She needed to eat. Rest. Recover.

She didn't need more bad news.

She didn't need another stress.

He couldn't keep the news from her, nor would he, but he didn't have to tell her now. There was nothing she could do. Nothing any of them could do.

He'd wait until they reached the palace to tell her about the call. Wait until she'd had a chance to shower and change and get something into her stomach because right now she looked on the verge of collapse.

"Shall we?" he asked, gesturing to the car.

CHAPTER FOUR

EMMELINE slowly rolled the cold water bottle between her hands, pretending to study the arid landscape, when in truth she was avoiding Makin's gaze.

She knew he was looking at her. Ever since they'd stopped alongside the road, he seemed quieter, grimmer, if such a thing were possible.

Earlier, by the side of the road, she'd thought she heard his phone ring but she'd only stepped around the car for a minute or two, so if he had talked to someone, it had been a short call.

Her sixth sense told her the call had something to do with her.

Maybe it was paranoia, but she had a cold, sinking sensation in her gut that told her he'd begun to put two and two together and things weren't adding up.

Had he figured out the truth? That she wasn't the real Hannah Smith?

Still worried, Emmeline saw a shimmer of green appear on the horizon. The shimmer of green gradually took shape, becoming trees and orchards as the desert gave way to a fertile oasis.

Fed by an underground stream that came from the mountains, the oasis became a city of red clay walls and narrow roads.

The sheikh's driver turned off the narrow highway onto an even narrower road shaded by tall date palms, the massive green-and-yellow fronds providing protection from the dazzling desert heat.

As the car approached the enormous gates ahead, they swung open, giving entrance into the walled city.

"Home," Makin said with quiet satisfaction as they traveled down yet another long drive bordered by majestic date palms, the heavy fronds like feathered plumes against the clear blue sky.

More gates opened and closed, revealing a sprawling building washed in the palest pink. But as the car continued to travel, Emmeline discovered the palace wasn't just one building, but a series of beautifully shaped buildings connected by trellises, patios, courtyards and gardens. No two were the same. Some had turrets and towers, others were domed, although each had the same smooth clay walls lushly covered in dark purple and white bougainvillea.

The car stopped before the tallest building, three stories tall with intricate gold-plated doors and massive gold, blue and white columns flanking the entrance.

Staff in billowy white pants and white jackets lined the entrance, smiling broadly and bowing low as Sheikh Al-Koury stepped from the car.

Having grown up in a palace, Emmeline was familiar with pomp, protocol and ceremony. Daily she'd witnessed the display of respect all were required to show the royal family, and yet there was something different about the sheikh's staff.

They greeted him with warmth and a genuine sense of pleasure in his return. They cared about him, and she saw from the way he responded to each man, he cared about them.

Makin paused at the ornate entrance, waiting for her, and together they stepped through the tall gold doors, leaving the bright sunlight and dazzling heat behind.

The serene, airy foyer was capped by a high domed ceiling of blue and gold, the cream walls stenciled in sophisticated gold swirls and elegant patterns. Emmeline drew a slow breath, relishing the palace's tranquility and delicious coolness. "Lovely," she said.

The sheikh lifted a brow, and glanced enquiringly at her.

She flushed, remembering she was supposed to be Hannah and familiar with everything here. "The coolness," she said. "Feels so good after the heat."

He stared down at her a moment, expression peculiar. He

seemed to be looking for something in her face, but what, she didn't know.

And then he nodded, a short nod, as if he'd come to a decision. "I'll walk you to your room," he said. "Make sure everything is as it should be."

Emmeline's brow puckered at his tone. Something *had* happened. She was sure of it.

He set off, leaving her to follow, and they crossed the spacious foyer, through one of the many exquisitely carved arches that opened off the entrance, their footsteps echoing on the limestone floor.

He turned down a hallway marked by ornamental columns. Sunlight streamed through high windows. Mosaic murals decorated the ivory walls and large ornate copper lanterns were hung from the high ceiling to provide light in the evening.

They passed through another arch which led outside to a rose-covered arbor. The roses were in full bloom, a soft luscious pink, and the heady scent reminded Emmeline of the formal rose garden at the palace in Brabant. She felt a sudden pang for all that she'd lose once her parents knew she wouldn't—couldn't—marry King Patek, and why. They'd be scandalized. They'd insist she'd get an abortion, something she wouldn't do.

There would be threats.

There would be anger.

Hostility.

Repercussions.

Makin paused before a beautiful door stained a rich mahogany and stepped aside for her to open it.

Hannah's room, she thought, opening the door to a spacious apartment contained in its own building. The high-ceilinged living room spoke of an understated elegance, the colors warmer here than in the rest of the palace. The living-room walls were pale gold and the furniture was gold with touches of red, ivory and blue. She glimpsed a bedroom off the living room with an attached bathroom. There was even a small kitchen where Hannah could prepare coffee and make simple meals.

"The cook made your favorite bread," he said, nodding at a

fabric-wrapped loaf on the tiled kitchen counter. "The refrigerator also has your yogurts and milk, and everything else you like. If you won't let Cook send you a tray for lunch, promise me you'll eat something right away."

She nodded. "I promise."

"Good." He hesitated, still standing just inside the doorway, clearly uncomfortable. "I need to tell you something. May we sit?"

She glanced at his face but his expression was shuttered, his silver gaze hard.

Emmeline walked to the low couch upholstered in a delicate silk the color of fresh butter, and moved some of the loose embroidered and jeweled pillows aside so she could sit down. He followed but didn't sit. He stood before her, arms crossed over his chest, his gray linen shirt pulled taut at the shoulders.

He was without a doubt a very handsome man. He radiated power and control, but right now he was scaring her with his fierce expression.

"There's been an accident," he said abruptly. "Last night on the way to the airport, Alejandro lost control of the car and crashed. Penelope died on the scene. Alejandro's in hospital."

It was the last thing Emmeline had expected him to say. She struggled to process what he'd just told her. Her mouth opened and closed without making a sound. She tried again. Failed.

"He was in surgery all night," Makin continued. "There was a lot of internal bleeding. His condition is extremely critical."

Reeling from shock, Emmeline clasped her hands tightly together, too stunned to speak.

Penelope was dead. Alejandro might not survive surgery. And yet both had been so beautiful and alive just hours ago.

Impossible.

Eyes burning, she gazed blindly out the glass doors to the garden beyond. Behind the walled garden the red mountains rose high, reminding her of the red dress Penelope had worn last night. And just like that, the desert was gone and all Emmeline could see was Penelope's vivid red dress against the billowing fabric of Alejandro's white shirt.

Her throat squeezed closed. Hot acid tears filmed her eyes. "Alejandro was...driving?" she asked huskily, finally finding her voice.

"He was at the wheel, yes."

"And Penelope?"

"Was thrown from the car on impact."

Emmeline closed her eyes, able to see it all and hating the movie reel of pictures in her head. Stupid, reckless Alejandro. Her heart ached for Penelope who was so young—just nineteen.

A tear fell, hot and wet on Emmeline's cheek. With a savage motion she brushed it away. She was furious. Furious with Alejandro. Furious that he took lives and wrecked them and threw them all away.

"I'm sorry, Hannah," Makin said, his deep voice rumbling through her. "I know you imagined yourself in love—"

"Please." Her voice broke and she lifted a hand to silence him. "Don't."

He crouched down before her, his powerful thighs all muscle, and caught her chin, forcing her to look at him. His silver-gray eyes glowed like pewter, hot and dark with emotion. "I know this isn't an easy time for you, but you'll survive this. I promise."

Then he surprised her by gently, carefully, sweeping his thumb across the curve of her cheek, catching the tears that fell. It was such a tender gesture from him, so kind and protective, it almost broke her heart.

She hadn't been touched so gently and kindly by anyone in years.

She'd never been touched by a man as if she mattered. "Thank you."

Makin stood. "You'll be all right," he repeated.

She wished she had an ounce of his confidence. "Yes." She wiped her eyes dry. "You're right. I'll shower and change and get to work." She rose, too, took several steps away to put distance between them. "What time shall I meet you?"

"I don't think you should try to do anything this afternoon."

"I know there must be stacks of mail—"

"And hundreds of emails, as well as dozens of phone messages all waiting for your attention, but they can wait a little longer," he said firmly. "I want you to take the rest of the day for yourself. Eat, sleep, read, go for a swim. Do whatever you need to do so that you can get back to work. I need your help, Hannah, but you're absolutely useless to me right now."

She felt her cheeks grow hot. "I'm sorry. I hate being a problem."

He gave her a peculiar look before his broad shoulders shifted. "Rest. Feel better. That would be the biggest help." Then he walked away, leaving her in the living room as if this was where she belonged.

But as the door closed behind him, she knew this wasn't where she belonged. It was where Hannah belonged.

These rooms, the food in the kitchen, the clothes in the closet…they were all Hannah's. Hannah needed her life back.

Emmeline glanced down at herself, feeling grimy and disheveled in her creased cocktail dress, and while she longed for a shower—and food—she had something more important to do first.

She had to reach Hannah. She'd put in calls yesterday but they'd all gone straight to voice mail. Hannah had texted her back, asking when Emmeline planned to arrive. Hannah was expecting Emmeline to show up in Raguva any moment to change places with her before anyone knew the difference. Which obviously wasn't going to happen.

Taking her phone from her small evening purse, Emmeline dialed Hannah's number, praying that she'd actually get through this time instead of reaching Hannah's voice mail again.

The phone rang and rang again before Hannah answered breathlessly. "Hello?"

Emmeline dragged a dark red embroidered pillow against her chest. "Hannah, it's me."

"I know. Are you okay?"

Emmeline squeezed the pillow tighter, her insides starting to churn. "I…I don't know."

"Are you coming here?"

"I…" Emmeline hesitated. "I…don't…know," she repeated,

stumbling a bit, feeling dishonest, because she knew the answer. She could never go to Raguva. Not now.

Tense silence stretched over the line and then Hannah asked tightly, "What do you mean, you don't know?"

Emmeline stared at the tall red mountains visible beyond the palace walls. She felt just as jagged as the mountain peaks. She'd flown all night, was seven weeks pregnant, and thousands of miles from Miami where Alejandro lay in critical condition. "I'm in Kadar."

Silence stretched over the line. "Kadar?" Hannah repeated wonderingly. "Why?"

Emmeline's shoulders rose, hunching. "Sheikh Al-Koury thinks I'm you."

Hannah exhaled hard. "Tell him you're not! Tell him the truth."

"I can't." Emmeline felt dangerously close to just losing it. It'd been such a difficult few weeks and she'd been so sure that she could turn things around, make it all right. But instead of things improving, they'd taken a dramatic turn for the worse. "I can't. Not before Sheikh Al-Koury's conference. It'd ruin everything."

"But everything's already ruined," Hannah cried, her voice rising and then breaking. "You have no idea what's happened—"

"I'm sorry, Hannah, I really am. But everything's out of my control."

"*Your* control. *Your* life. It's always about you, isn't it?"

"I didn't mean it that way—"

"But you did mean to send me here in your place and you didn't intend to come right away. You used me. Manipulated me. But how do you think I feel being trapped here, pretending to—" Hannah broke off abruptly.

The line went dead.

Hannah had hung up.

Emmeline stared at the phone, stunned. But what did she expect? She had done an amazing job of messing up Hannah's life.

Makin had met briefly with his staff after leaving Hannah's room and spent fifteen minutes in his office listening to updates from his various department managers before dismissing them all with a wave of his hand.

He couldn't focus on the updates. His thoughts were elsewhere, back with Hannah in her room.

Telling Hannah about Alejandro's accident had been far harder than he'd imagined. He hadn't liked giving her bad news. It didn't feel right. He'd never felt protective of her before, but he did now.

Maybe it was because she wasn't well.

Maybe it was knowing she'd had her heart broken.

Maybe it's because he was suddenly aware of her in a way he hadn't been before.

Aware of her as a woman. Aware that she was very much a woman. A highly desirable woman. And that was a problem.

Mouth compressing, he rose from behind his desk, left his office and set off to meet the Kasbah's director of security, who had promised to give him a tour of the guest wings and go over the security measures in place for the safety of their guests.

The tour was interrupted by a phone call with information that Alejandro was out of surgery and in recovery. He hadn't woken yet, and while the prognosis was still grim, he'd at least survived the nine-hour operation. For Hannah's sake, he was glad.

Call concluded, he and the security director passed through a high, arched doorway and stepped outside. "Which families will be in that building?" he asked, struggling to get his attention back on his life, his work, his conference. He wasn't a man who was easily distracted, but he seemed unable to focus on anything other than Hannah right now.

"The Nuris of Baraka, Your Highness. Sultan Malek Nuri and his brother Sheikh Kalen Nuri, along with their wives. Sheikh Tair of Ohua."

"And in the building to my right?"

"Our Western dignitaries."

Makin nodded. "Good." He was relieved to see that not only was security prepared, but the Kasbah looked immaculate.

While all of Makin's various homes and palaces were beautiful, Kasbah Raha always took his breath away. The Kasbah itself was hundreds of years old, and lovingly preserved by genera-

tions of the Al-Koury family, the colors mirroring the desert—
the pink of sunrise, the majestic red mountains, the blue of the
sky, and the ivory-and-gold sand.

It was remote. And it was the place he worked best. Which is
why he'd never brought Madeline to Raha. Raha was for clarity
of thought and personal reflection...not desire or lust. He'd never
wanted to associate a carnal pleasure such as sex with Raha,
either, but suddenly, with Hannah under his roof, he was thinking
about very carnal things instead of focusing on the conference.

Hannah.

Just saying her name made his insides tighten.

And that twinge of tension was enough for him to come to
a decision.

This wasn't going to work with her here. He realized they'd
only just arrived, but she had to go. The timing was terrible, but
there was too much at risk to allow himself to be mired in in-
decision.

CHAPTER FIVE

STILL flattened from her call to Hannah, Emmeline showered and wrapped herself in her robe that had been unpacked and hung in the closet next to Hannah's wardrobe.

Curious, Emmeline sorted through Hannah's clothes. Hannah's wardrobe wasn't exactly dowdy, but it was practical. Hannah dressed conservatively in keeping with her job.

Stretching out on the bed, Emmeline felt a sudden rush of affection for her lookalike, thinking Hannah was the kind of friend you'd want in your corner. And she'd been in Emmeline's corner, too...

Emmeline didn't remember drifting off to sleep, but hours later the doorbell woke her.

Sitting up, she saw the sun had shifted across the sky and now sat low, hinting at twilight. Pale violet shadows crept across the bedroom and hovered in corners. She headed for the door. One of the palace's kitchen staff stood outside with a gleaming silver trolley.

"Good evening, Miss Smith," the palace staffer greeted her. "His Highness thought you'd want to dine tonight in the privacy of your own room."

A thoughtful gesture on the sheikh's part, she thought, opening the door wider. The man pushed the trolley through the living room out onto the flagstone patio. Emmeline watched as he arranged the tables and chairs closer to the pool and covered the small round table with a cloth from the cart, then dishes, silverware, goblets, candles and a low floral arrangement.

Then with a brief respectful nod to Emmeline, he left, taking the now-empty cart with him. Once he was gone, Emmeline stepped out onto the patio. The table had been set for two. Two plates, two sets of silverware, two water and two wine goblets.

She wasn't dining alone tonight.

And just like that, Emmeline's sense of well-being fled.

The moment Hannah opened the door that evening, Makin knew he'd made a mistake. He should have called her to his office to tell her he was sending her away, summoning her as one would summon an employee, instead of breaking the news over dinner.

He'd thought that talking in private would lessen the blow. But he was wrong. Wrong to speak to her at dinner, in her room.

Worse, she'd dressed for dinner tonight, and she'd never dressed for dinner before.

Why had she put on a frothy cocktail dress? And why those gold high heels that made her legs look silky smooth and endless?

Makin followed her slowly through her gold living room to the garden knowing he was compounding matters, adding insult to injury by staying. One didn't give employees bad news like this. He should go and wait until the morning. Go and wait until he felt calmer, more settled.

But he didn't leave. He couldn't, not when he felt an irresistible pull to stay. Instead of going, he trailed after her through the large sliding glass doors to the garden where a table had been set for two.

Makin's gaze rested on the table and his unease grew.

She'd dressed to match the table setting, her orange chiffon gown a darker, more vibrant shade than the table's rich apricot-and-gold jeweled cloth. Tall tapered candles framed the low floral centerpiece of apricot and cream roses.

Yet another mistake. His chief of staff had misunderstood him.

Makin blamed himself for the confusion. He should have been more clear with his kitchen and waiting staff. He'd requested a quiet meal with Hannah so he could speak frankly with her. He'd asked to have the meal served in her room so he could talk without interruption. It had never crossed his mind that his simple request would get turned into this....

This...

Intimate setting for two.

Makin frowned at the gleaming display of silver, crystal wine goblets and fine bone china.

His frown turned grim as the tall tapered candles flickered and danced, throwing shadows and light across the table, accenting the rich jewel tones of the embroidered cloth. More candles flickered in hammered iron wall sconces. Even the pool and fountain were softly lit as a whisper of a breeze rustled through the tall date palms standing sentry around the perimeter of the garden.

Makin had come to Hannah's apartment hundreds of times over the years, but they'd never dined here before, not alone, not late at night, and certainly never like this.

When they met for dinner, the tone had always been professional, the focus centered on business. She'd attended numerous banquets with him. Had sat across from him at countless perfunctory meals where she took notes and he rattled off instructions. But it had never been this, never the two of them seated across from each other dining by moonlight and candlelight. The lighting changed everything, as did the soft sheen of the embroidered silk tablecloth. The shimmer of fabric, the glow of light created intimacy...sensuality.

She'd never met him in anything but tailored jackets and skirts and demure blouses before, either. And yet she'd dressed tonight. As if this wasn't just a business dinner. As if this was something more...something personal...as if this was a...date.

Just the thought of being alone with Hannah on a date, in a filmy cocktail dress and high strappy gold heels, made him harden.

It was a good thing he'd made the decision this afternoon to send her to a different office to work with different people. A good thing he'd decided to act swiftly. Relationships were tricky, particularly in the work arena, and he'd always been very careful to keep business and personal separate. But now, with Hannah, the line between work and personal life felt blurred. Around

Hannah he'd begun to crave…something. And Makin was not a man to crave anything.

"We need to talk," he said roughly, gesturing to the table, deciding he wouldn't wait for dinner to say what he needed to say. He'd just do it right away. Get it over with. He wouldn't be able to relax until he'd broken the news and she'd accepted his decision.

He watched as Hannah sat down gracefully, obediently, at the table and looked up at him, waiting for him to speak. On one hand she was doing everything right—sitting quietly, waiting patiently—and yet everything felt wrong.

Starting with her orange chiffon cocktail dress. And the gold bangle on her wrist. And the fact that she had left her long thick hair loose about her shoulders.

How could he coldly announce he was sending her away, transferring her to another department, when she was looking so good and lovely?

Especially lovely. The *lovely* part frustrated him. He felt tricked. Played.

Hannah didn't wear vivid colors like juicy orange or exotic peacock. She didn't leave her hair loose or smudge her eyes with eyeliner or stain her lips with soft pink color.

He turned his back on her to face the pool. The rectangular blue pool was illuminated tonight with small spotlights aimed at the elegant fountain so that shadows of dancing water played across the back wall. But even the small spotlights hinted at intimacy.

Makin walked around the edge of the pool, ran a troubled hand across his jaw, unable to remember a time when he'd been this uncomfortable. The night was warm but it wasn't the temperature making him miserable. It was the knowledge that this was his last night with Hannah, that tomorrow he'd be sending her away.

He knew it was for the best but still…

Makin rolled his shoulders, trying to release the tension balled in the muscles between his shoulder blades. Even his white shirt felt too snug against his shoulders and his trousers hot against his skin.

"You're making me nervous," she said quietly, her voice soft in the warm night.

He glanced at her, still unable to make sense of this Hannah, or of his ambivalent feelings for her.

For four and a half years they'd worked closely together and as much as he'd valued her and appreciated her skill, he'd never felt the least bit attracted to her. There had never been chemistry. Nor did he want there to be. She was an employee. Intelligent, productive and useful. Three words he used to describe his laptop, too. But you didn't take a computer to bed.

"Why?" he asked equally quietly, seeing the faint tremble of her soft lower lip, and then the pinch of her teeth as they bit down.

The bite of her teeth into that tender pink lip made him hot, blisteringly hot. It was a physical heat, a heat that made him harden and his temper stir.

This was absurd. Ridiculous. Why was he feeling things now? Why was he responding to her now? For God's sake, he was her boss. She was dependent on him. One didn't take advantage of one's position or power in life. Not ever. That lesson had been drummed into him from a very early age.

And yet his hard, heavy erection was very real, as was his drumming pulse.

He was feeling very angry, very annoyed and very impatient. With her, with him, with all of this.

"Something is obviously wrong," she said, sitting tall and still, her slender hands folded in her lap.

His body ached. His erection throbbed. His blood felt like hot, spiced wine, and he was on edge, the night suddenly erotic, electric.

He told himself it was the candlelight and the moon—pale gold and three-quarters full. It was the warm breeze in the palms teasing his senses, making him more restless than usual.

But it wasn't the soft glow of light, or the breeze or the rich, musky scent of roses, but her.

Hannah.

He was absolutely sure he was doing the right thing in sending her to London in the morning. He wouldn't allow doubts to

creep in or cloud his thinking. She'd like the London division.
She'd be an asset there. By tomorrow afternoon she'd be installed
in her new office, meeting her new team, and knowing Hannah,
she'd settle in quickly.

But somehow it seemed wrong to break the news to her like
this, now, when she looked so beautiful that she took his breath
away.

"That's a new dress," he said curtly, his tone almost accusa-
tory.

Bewildered by the sharpness in his voice, her brows pulled
together. "No. It's not new. I've had it for a while."

"I've never seen it."

She ran a light hand across her lap, as if smoothing imagi-
nary wrinkles from the silky chiffon. "I haven't ever worn it
around you before."

"Why now?"

Her lips pursed and she looked at him strangely. "I can go
change if you'd like." She started to rise. "I didn't realize the
dress would upset you—"

"It hasn't."

"You're angry."

"I'm not."

"I'll put on something else—"

"Sit." His deep voice rumbled through the garden, sounding
too loud as it bounced and echoed off the high garden walls. *It's
not her fault,* he told himself. She hadn't done anything wrong.
He was the one who'd decided to send her away. She hadn't asked
to go. "Please," he added more quietly.

She sank back into her chair, her wide lavender-blue gaze
wary.

He closed the distance between them, leaned on the back of his
chair and struggled to find the right words. The words that would
allow him to put her on the plane to Heathrow tomorrow with
the least amount of drama possible. He hated drama. Hated tears.

But closer to her wasn't better. Closer just made him more
aware of how very appealing she was.

The pleated orange-chiffon gown left her slim, pale shoulders bare. The dress's neckline was hidden by a wide gold collar. And with her long dark hair loose and her eyes rimmed in a smoky gray, she looked like an exotic princess from a children's story-book. He could almost imagine she was waiting for the brave knight, the noble prince, who could sweep her away, give her that storybook ending.

If he were the sort of royal who believed in that sort of thing.

Which he wasn't. He didn't. He was too practical. Too driven. Too ambitious. He had a purpose in life. A mission. It wasn't enough that he be a great leader for his people. His personal mission was bigger than the borders of Kadar. His mission was to help the world.

It sounded grandiose. Perhaps it even made him sound a bit like a prig. But if his father could accomplish what he had with a brutal degenerative disease, then Makin could accomplish even more.

He had to.

The world was polluting itself to death, choking on chemi-cals and strangling on debt. The rich were getting richer and the poor, sick and hungry were still suffering and dying at a stag-gering rate.

For the past five years he'd met privately with powerful, wealthy visionaries from the music industry and high-tech busi-nesses, to pool resources and make an even greater impact around the world. The goal was to get clean water to all people, to help immunize children in all third-world countries, to provide mos-quito nets to help protect all vulnerable people from malaria.

Food. Shelter. Education. Safety.

For all children, regardless of religion, race, culture or gen-der. This was his goal. This was his life's ambition. And this was why he was sending her away.

She'd become a distraction. A liability. And nothing could come between him and his work.

"Sheikh Al-Koury, are you firing me?"

Her uncertain voice broke the silence.

He turned his head, glanced at her, felt a dull ache in his chest. Damn her. Damn the garden. Damn the moonlight and the orange floaty fabric of her dress that clung to her small, firm breasts and made him want things he couldn't want with her.

"Yes," he said roughly. "No. Not firing. It's a transfer."

"Transfer to where?"

"The London office."

"But I live in Dallas."

"You've always enjoyed London."

"But my home—"

"Will now be London." His gaze met hers. He steeled himself, reminding himself that the only way to pull this off was to be ruthless. Hard. "If you no longer wish to work for me, I understand. But if you do, you'll embrace the challenges of your new position in the marketing and public relations department for the international division."

There. He'd said it. Makin exhaled. For the first time in days he felt relief. He felt in control again.

Silence stretched. The only sound in the garden was the bubble and splash of the fountain and the swish and whisper of palm fronds overhead.

Hannah's smooth jaw shifted, her lips compressed, but still she said nothing, which provoked him. She worked for him, not the other way around. It was her job to accept. Acquiesce. To make this change comfortable and easy for all of them.

"It's a promotion," he said tautly. "Human resources will provide you with temporary housing until you find something you like—"

"I like my job here, with you."

"You're needed elsewhere now."

"Yesterday you needed me here."

"Things change."

Her lips parted ever so slightly as if realizing where this was going, and why.

He hoped she'd gracefully fold, accept his new plan for her. He needed her to concede.

Her gaze turned beseeching. "Alejandro was a mistake. I admit I made a mistake—"

"It has nothing to do with Alejandro—"

"It has everything to do with Alejandro," she cried.

"You're wrong," he countered, torn between wanting to comfort her and crush her because all she needed to do was accept. Give. Agree. Not fight. Not cry. Not make him feel an ounce more emotion tonight.

"I'm not stupid," she said, eyes still shimmering but now flashing with bright hot sparks.

"No, you aren't."

"Then why?" She leaned forward, cheeks flushed, breasts rising and falling with every quick breath. "For four years I have given you everything. For four years I have made your goals mine. For four years I have put your needs before mine. I don't take vacations. I don't use sick days. I don't have a social life. I don't even have a fashionable wardrobe. My life is all about you, and only you."

"All the more reason you need to go to London."

She shot him a withering look, a look that should have cooled his hunger, but it didn't, and he couldn't remember when he'd last felt this way—so raw and physical, so completely carnal.

Before French-born Madeline had been his mistress there had been Jenny, a stunning English woman, and like Madeline, she'd been slim and blonde and very bright. He'd always been attracted to blonde, intelligent women. He took care of his mistresses, too, financially, and physically. When he made love with his mistress, he made sure she was pleasured. He wanted her happy. But he didn't offer love. Nor would he.

It wasn't her fault, he'd told Madeline more than once. It was his. He wasn't sensitive. Wasn't the type to feel certain emotions. Wasn't the type to feel passion.

And yet at the moment Makin literally felt as if he was on fire, his skin hot, nerves sensitive, his body rippling with tension and need. It wasn't rational. And far from civilized. He wanted to grab her, shake her—

He broke off with a shake of his own head. Madness. He'd never wanted to shake a woman before, or drag her from her chair and into his arms. He didn't lose control. Didn't feel strong emotions. So what was happening to him now?

"There will be a bump in your salary, as well as better benefits," he said. "Including another week of vacation."

Her lips curved. "Another week to add to the weeks and months I've never used?"

"Perhaps it's time you started taking those holidays."

"Perhaps it is."

Her tart tone made him see red. Sassy, saucy wench. How dare she speak to him with that attitude? How dare she smirk at him from beneath those long, black lashes as if he was the problem, not she?

What the hell was happening to him? He didn't even know himself at the moment. His shaft ached and throbbed and his hands itched to reach for her, catch her by the wrist and pull her toward him so that he could take her mouth, cover that mocking twist of her lips with his and make her his.

It wasn't a desire but a need. To know her. Feel her. Make her part of him.

His fingers flexed and balled before returning to hard fists. Clearly he wasn't himself.

He wasn't an aggressive man, and he didn't drag women about, and he didn't teach them lessons, but right now he wanted to remind her who he was, and what he was and how he wasn't a man to be trifled with.

He was Sheikh Makin Al-Koury, one of the world's most powerful men. He had a plan and a vision and nothing distracted him from it.

Certainly not his secretary. She was disposable. Dispensable. Replaceable. And he'd proved it by swiftly organizing the job transfer to London.

"So why this…promotion…now?" she asked, her gaze meeting his and holding, expression challenging.

"I'm ready for a change. And I think you are, too."

Her eyes sparked blue fire. Her eyebrows lifted. "How kind of you to think for me."

"That's not what I meant."

"Good, and I respectfully ask that you don't make decisions

for me based on what you think I need. You do not know me. You know nothing about me—"

"That's actually not respectful. And I do know you. I know virtually everything about you."

She laughed. Out loud. Practically in his face.

"If you knew me, Your Highness," she drawled his title, "you'd know who I am." She paused a moment, lashes dropping, concealing the hot bright blue of her eyes. "And who I am not."

Maybe he shouldn't transfer her to London. Maybe he should fire her. Her impudence was galling. He wouldn't have accepted this blatant lack of respect from anyone but her.

"You go too far," he thundered. He hadn't actually raised his voice, but his tone was so hard and fierce that it silenced her immediately.

She fell back into her seat, shoulders tense, lips pressed thinly. For a moment he imagined he saw pain in her eyes and then it was gone, replaced by a stony chill.

"I'm trying to help you," he said quietly.

She looked away, her gaze settling on the bubbling fountain. "You're trying to get rid of me."

"Maybe I am."

And there it was. The truth. Spoken aloud.

He'd said it and he saw by the way she flinched she'd heard it, too.

For a long, endless moment they sat in silence, she staring at the blue ceramic fountain while he stared at her, drinking in her profile, memorizing the delicate, elegant lines of her face. He'd never appreciated her beauty before, had never seen the high-winged eyebrow, the prominent thrust of her cheekbone, the full, sensual curve of her lips.

His chest grew tight, a spasm of intense sensation. Regret. A whisper of pain. He would miss her.

"Is that it, then?" she asked, turning her head to look at him, dark hair spilling across her shoulder and over the soft ripe chiffon of her orange dress. She was staring deeply into his eyes as if she were trying to see straight through him, into the very heart of him.

He let her look, too, knowing she couldn't see anything, knowing she, like everyone else, only saw what he allowed people to see…

Which was nothing.

Nothing but distance. And hollow space.

Years ago knowing that his father was dying and that his mother didn't want to live without his father, he'd constructed the wall around his emotions, burying his heart behind brick and mortar. No one, not even Madeline, was given access to his emotions. No one was ever allowed that close.

"Is that why we're here having dinner?" she added. "Is that what you came here tonight to say?"

"Yes."

She looked at him for another long, unnerving moment, her eyes a brilliant, startling blue against the paleness of her face. "All right." She shrugged lightly, almost indifferently, and rose to her feet. "Am I excused then?"

"Dinner hasn't even been served."

"I don't think I could stomach a bite now, and it seems a waste of time to sit and make small talk when I could begin getting organized for my flight tomorrow."

CHAPTER SIX

"Dinner hasn't been served," he repeated calmly, leaning back in his chair, stretching out his legs, his broad shoulders square.

Emmeline gazed down at him, thinking that if one didn't know him, one might think he was a gorgeous, easygoing man, the kind of man you'd want to take home to meet the family.

But she did know him. And he was gorgeous but he wasn't easy, or simple or kind.

He was fierce and intimidating and totally overwhelming.

But she was supposed to be Hannah, and Hannah was supposed to like him, even though he'd just transferred her to a new position in London.

"I'm sure the kitchen could send the meal to you in your rooms since I no longer want to eat," she said, masking her anger with her most royal, serene expression.

His dark head tipped, black hair like onyx in the candlelight. "I'm not going to have my staff chasing me all over the palace with a dinner cart," he replied cordially. "I planned to eat here with you. And I will eat here." He paused, and then smiled but the warmth in his eyes was dangerous, as if he were not entirely civilized. "And so will you."

She'd never seen that look in his eye before. Had never thought of him as anything but coldly sophisticated, an elegant Arab sheikh with far too much money and power. But right now he practically hummed with aggression. It was strange—and disorienting.

Emmeline braced herself against the edge of the table with

its opulent settings and gleaming candlelight. Her legs shook beneath her. "You can't force me to eat."

"No, I can't force you. And so I'm asking you. Would you please sit down and join me for dinner? I'm hungry, and I know you've eaten virtually nothing today, and a good meal wouldn't hurt you. You're far too thin these days. You don't eat enough—"

"If I stay and eat, would you at least reconsider your decision to send me to London?"

"No," he answered bluntly. "My decision has been made."

"But you can change it."

"I won't. I stand by my decision. It is the right one."

"Please." Her voice dropped to a husky note and broke. "Please. I don't want to go to London—"

"Hannah."

"I'll do better. I'll work harder." Her voice cracked. "It doesn't seem fair to just throw me away after four years—"

"I am not throwing you away!" He was on his feet and starting toward her but then stopped himself. "And don't beg. You've no reason to beg. It's beneath you, especially when you've done nothing wrong."

"If I haven't done anything wrong, why am I being sent away?"

"Because sometimes change is necessary."

Emmeline's heart felt as if it was breaking. She'd failed Hannah again. She reached up to wipe a tear away before it fell. Her hand was trembling so hard that she missed the tear and had to try again.

"Don't."

"What? I'm not allowed to hurt? To have emotions? I'm supposed to just let you send me away as if I don't care?"

"Yes."

"Why?"

"Because your job is to make my life easier and you're not."

"How terrible."

"But true."

She struggled to catch another tear. "I didn't realize I wasn't allowed to be human—"

"I realize you're disappointed, but this isn't personal, and I'd like you to remain professional. So if you could pull yourself together and have a seat—"

"No."

His nostrils flared. A small muscle popped in his jaw. "No?" he repeated, his voice velvet-soft. "Did I hear you correctly?"

Her lower lip quivered. "Yes."

He moved toward her, a deep hard line between his black eyebrows. "That's insubordination, Miss Smith."

"I won't be bullied."

"I'm not a bully, I'm your boss." He was before her now, and standing so close that she had to tip her head back to see his face. "Or have you forgotten?"

She'd always thought his eyes were a cool silver-gray, but with him just inches away, she could see that his eyes burned and glowed like molten pewter.

"Haven't forgotten," she whispered, her courage starting to fade, as he dwarfed her, not just in height, but in sheer size. His shoulders were immense, his chest broad, his body muscular and strong. But he overpowered her in other ways—made her feel fragile and foolish and terribly emotional.

"Perhaps you'd care to apologize?"

There was a lethal quality to his voice, a leashed tension in his stance. It crossed her mind that she'd pushed him too far, demanded too much. "I'm sorry."

"Sorry for what?" His voice was so rough and deep it sounded like a growl.

She was mesmerized by the tiny gold flecks in his gray eyes. That's why up close his eyes looked warmer. His eyes weren't a cold gray. They had bits of the desert's gold sun and sand in them. "I've botched it all up." Her voice dropped and the air caught in her lungs. "Again."

He was silent, and then he gave his head the slightest of shakes. "I can't do this with you."

She squeezed her eyes closed, nodded her head.

"But I do accept your apology," he added.

Eyes still closed, she nodded again.

"Hannah."

She couldn't look at him, she couldn't, not when she was so overwhelmed by everything.

"Hannah, open your eyes."

"I can't."

"Why not?"

"Because you'll see…you'll see…"

"What?" he demanded, tipping her chin up with a finger.

She opened her eyes, looked up at him, her vision blurred by tears. "Me."

For a long, endless moment he simply stared into her eyes. "And why would that be a bad thing?"

The unexpected tenderness in his voice made her heart seize. "Because you don't like me."

He exhaled hard. "That's where you're wrong."

"Am I?"

"Absolutely." And then his head abruptly dropped, blocking the moon, and his lips covered hers.

It was the last thing she'd expected. The last thing she wanted. She froze, her lips stiff beneath his. For a second she even forgot how to breathe, and the air bottled in her lungs until her head began to spin and little dots danced before her eyes.

His lips traveled slowly across hers, in a light, fleeting kiss that was more comfort than passion. Her back tingled. She shivered and lifted a hand to press against his chest, intending to push him away, and yet her hand seemed to like the feel of his chest, her palm absorbing his warmth, her fingers splaying against the smooth, dense plane of muscle that wrapped his ribs.

Emmeline found herself leaning forward, drawn to his warmth and the heady spice of his cologne and the coolness of his mouth on hers. He nipped lightly at her lower lip, coaxing a response from her and sending a frisson of feeling zipping up her spine. Emmeline shuddered with pleasure, lips parting slightly with a muffled gasp.

Makin's arm wrapped around her waist, drawing her close so that his hard frame pressed against the length of her. He was powerfully built, hard and muscular, and heat radiated from him in waves.

Teasingly his tongue parted the seam of her lips, sending a shock of hot, electric sensation throughout her. She shuddered again, her lips parting beneath his, as her breasts grew heavy, aching, nipples exquisitely sensitive.

She'd never been kissed like this, never felt anything remotely like this. Makin's mouth tasted of spearmint and his spicy cologne filled her nose and his hard jaw was smooth, the skin soft from a recent shave. Her senses swam with the pleasure of it all.

Again he traced the seam of her lips with the tip of his tongue so that she gasped, opening her mouth wider for him. His tongue slid across her soft inner lip even as she felt his hand in the small of her back, a slow, leisurely stroke down over her hips. The lazy caress sent a hot new streak of sensation through her. It felt as if he was spreading fire beneath her skin. She tingled and ached, her womb tightening in need, and she lifted her hands to clasp his face, kissing him back, feeling more urgency.

Makin responded by deepening the kiss, his tongue delving into her mouth to taste her, his lips biting at hers, moving across hers, making every nerve dance to life. She gasped and arched, her hips pressing helplessly against his, making her aware of his thick hot erection. The rub of his erection between her thighs turned her legs to jelly, making her weak.

She'd only been kissed by Alejandro before, and it was that night he'd taken her virginity. His kiss had been hard, and she'd felt no lick of fire in her veins, no deep hot ache between her thighs. She'd felt pressure. A grating and grinding of jaw, lips, tongue and teeth. But there was no grating of anything here. No, Makin was making her melt, dissolving her bones into puddles of thick sweet honey.

Honey of want. Honey of need.

He was driving her wild. He slowly swept his hand back up her bottom to cup the curve of her breast, the palm of his hand so warm against her sensitive skin. She pressed closer wanting a satisfaction she couldn't even name, her fingers tangling, tightening in his shirt.

She heard a hoarse, desperate moan and then realized it was her. She'd whimpered aloud, and if she heard it, he did, too.

Heat rushed through her, a rush of embarrassment and she started to pull away and then his hand found her breast, his fingers catching, kneading the taut nipple and she shuddered and curled back against him, hips, breasts, thighs pressed to him, giving herself over to the hot, intense sensation.

He could have her, she thought, as he sucked the tip of her tongue into his mouth and drew on it, a slow, sensual rhythm that made her pulse throb and her knees press together. She felt hot and wet, her satin thong slick against the softness between her thighs.

He made a rough sound, a sound both primal and male, as he caught the back of her head in his hand, holding her still to kiss her more deeply.

She was drowning in desire, overwhelmed by need. And as he took her mouth, she didn't think she'd ever felt quite so frantic. He could do anything he wanted with her. He could do anything as long as he didn't stop touching her, didn't stop tasting her. She'd never felt so much sensation, never felt such sweet, wild pleasure. He could lift her onto the table and press her against the dishes and cutlery, crushing her into the flowers and she wouldn't protest. He could lift the hem of her dress and slide his fingers beneath the satin edge of her thong and between her thighs where she ached and ached.

He could fill her.

He could.

And then she felt his hand draw the chiffon fabric up over her thigh, and his fingers slide across warm bare skin. She shuddered, and reached up to clasp his nape, and then grab at the ends of his dark, thick hair.

She was empty, so unbearably wet and empty, and she needed him to warm her, needed him to fill her, needed—

"No."

It was just one word, one syllable, and yet he said it loudly, harshly, as he pulled her hands from around his neck and pushed her back, setting her away from him.

"No," he repeated thickly, dark color high in his cheekbones, his breathing still ragged. "I can't do this."

She heard what he was saying but couldn't seem to think of an appropriate response, not when her blood still hummed in her veins and her body felt hot and wet, and there was that terrible ache between her legs.

She'd never known physical desire, had never been truly aroused, and yet all of a sudden she understood why teenagers sat in parked cars and how good girls got themselves into trouble.

They lost control because what they felt was so good.

They forgot the dangers because pleasure could be so addictive.

"That shouldn't have happened," he added. "I apologize. It won't happen again."

"It's okay—"

"No. No, it's not. It's wrong. I have a mistress. I don't want this from you."

And then he left her without a second glance.

Stunned, she slid into the nearest chair, her hands falling numbly to her sides.

She felt shattered.

Even now she could feel the dizzying heat of the kiss, and the scorching warmth of Makin's hard body against hers. She could still smell the tantalizing hint of his fragrance lingering in the air—or was it on her skin? It was a scent of sandalwood and spice, a smell that reminded her of this desert of his—warm, exotic, golden.

But then his words returned to her, *No. I don't want this from you,* and she cringed with shame, and the gorgeous pleasure faded away.

His words hurt.

Exhaling slowly, trying to stop the rush of pain, she got to her feet, took a step, and then another, until she was walking around the pool. For several minutes she just made herself move. It was easier when she was moving not to feel so much. Not to hurt so much. Easier to work through his bruising disdain.

And then finally, when she'd walked herself to a place of

quiet and calm, she was able to tell herself that the sheikh had overreacted.

It was a kiss, just a kiss, nothing more. He might be upset but there had been no great impropriety. They hadn't undressed, they weren't lying down, hadn't touched intimately.

And yet…

She stopped, ran a hand along her neck and down to the valley between her breasts. It had been a hot, explosive kiss. A kiss that had seared her, burned her, made her understand what she wanted from a man.

Hunger. Fire. Passion. All the things she'd been taught to believe were bad, wicked…and yet when she was in his arms, it hadn't felt wicked. It had felt sweet.

She'd felt good. Beautiful and strong and lovely. Emmeline rarely felt lovely. The world heralded her as her generation's great beauty but she didn't feel beautiful. She'd never felt like anything special until just now….

Biting her lip, she turned away, confused. Conflicted.

How could something that felt so good be wrong?

When she'd been in Makin's arms she hadn't felt any shame, any guilt, nothing but pleasure. And she refused to feel shame now. She wouldn't let the kiss become ugly, wouldn't let the dizzying pleasure turn to disgust.

Swallowing hard, she smoothed the silky chiffon hem of her dress over the heated skin of her upper thigh. Just the whisper of fabric against her sensitive skin made her insides turn over and her breasts tighten as she was flooded with another scalding rush of desire.

This is how good girls go bad, she thought ruefully, slipping one gold high-heeled sandal off, and then the other. This is how eligible ladies ruined their chances. Not on men like Alejandro, men who kissed too hard with their jaws and tongues, but men like Makin who could make a woman feel wonderful and beautiful inside and out.

And even though Makin Al-Koury had hurt her after with his harsh rejection, the kiss itself had been amazing.

The kiss had made her feel amazing. As though she'd actually mattered.

Smiling wistfully, she picked up the shoes by the thin gold straps and rose. Leaning across the table, Emmeline blew out the candles, one by one, and then, shoes in hand, headed into Hannah's apartment.

She was sliding the glass doors closed when the doorbell chimed. Had Makin returned?

"Good evening, Miss Smith," the uniformed kitchen staff greeted her as she opened the door. "Sheikh Al-Koury is taking his dinner in his own room, but said you'd want something to eat."

Emmeline's smile slipped.

That was the moment she remembered that the kiss, so good and melting and bittersweet, hadn't been meant for her. Makin thought he'd kissed Hannah Smith.

The kiss—the one he'd regretted—had been for Hannah. But if he regretted kissing Hannah, his perfect secretary, how would he react if he knew he'd kissed Emmeline d'Arcy, the princess he despised?

Emmeline choked back a strangled laugh. Her eyes stung and burned. She swallowed once and again. And then she did what she'd been taught to do her entire life—she arranged her features into a formal but polite smile—and graciously thanked the kind kitchen staff for bringing her dinner.

That kiss, he thought, *that kiss...*

It was two-thirty in the morning and Makin was still up, his thoughts unusually chaotic, and he climbed from bed, giving up the illusion of trying to sleep.

He was angry he'd kissed her, angry with himself, angry with his loss of control.

He never lost control.

And that kiss...

It threatened to change everything. It had made him feel things he didn't feel. Hadn't thought he could feel. Holding her, tasting her had been intoxicating. He'd felt like someone else. Someone different.

He'd felt.

And suddenly he didn't want to send her away, on to London and a new position, but he wanted to keep her here, for him, with him. Not as his assistant but as his woman.

But he had a woman. He had Madeline. And until tonight he'd been happy with her as his mistress.

Had been, he silently repeated, brow furrowing, his expression darkening as he paced the length of his bedroom once and again.

Why was he so tempted by Hannah? Was Madeline not enough for him anymore?

Skin hot, emotions hotter, Makin opened the tall glass doors and walked out onto his balcony. Moonlight turned the garden below silver and white. A fountain splashed and he leaned against the elegant iron railing, aware that his attraction to Hannah was stronger than anything he'd ever felt for Madeline or Jenny or any woman in years.

But then, he'd always deliberately chosen beautiful women who were cool and calm…composed. His mistresses accommodated him, never challenging him or disturbing his focus.

Everything about Hannah disturbed his focus.

He shouldn't like it, shouldn't allow it. He'd never wanted fire or intensity with his women before. He was too practical. He wanted convenience, companionship and satisfaction. And he had all that with Madeline. When in Nadir he saw her two, maybe three times, a week. If she chafed at their limited time together, she never said so. She greeted him with smiles and easy warmth, and there was never pressure to be anything but present. It was enough. Enough for her, enough for him.

He liked their routine in Nadir. He'd join her around nine or ten in the evening. They'd have dinner, a little conversation, sex, and then he'd return home. He never stayed the night. He never wanted to. And it was the kind of relationship that worked for him.

What kind of mistress would Hannah be? He pictured installing her in a beautiful house overlooking the royal gardens in Nadir, pictured working all day then going to her at night.

Pictured her opening the door, wearing something orange and filmy, or perhaps a sleek black satin evening gown with a thigh-high slit up the front. Makin hardened.

He wouldn't want dinner. Or talk. He'd want her. Immediately. He'd want to take her there in the hall, slip his hands beneath the fabric and find her soft sensitive skin and make her shudder and whimper against him.

And then he'd want her again in the bedroom, beneath him on the bed, pale thighs parted, her breasts rising and falling as he rose up over her, plunging slowly, deeply into her, filling her, making her cry out his name.

Body aching, shaft throbbing, Makin turned, leaned against the railing and gazed into his bedroom glowing with yellow light, wishing Hannah were in his bed now. He wanted her now. Needed her, needed release.

His hand slipped down his belly, reaching into his loose pajama pants to grip his heavy erection. He palmed himself once, twice, his grip firm as he pictured her blue eyes, the curve of her lips, the firmness of her breasts and the ripeness of her hips and ass.

He would take her from behind, and then flip her over, and take her again, this time drawing her down onto his shaft so that he could watch her face as he made her come.

He wanted to make her come. He wanted to make her come over and over…

Madness.

This was exactly why he had to send her away. He didn't want to feel this much for a woman, didn't want to become emotionally involved. He had a job to do, a plan for his future, a plan that didn't include sex in hallways and restless nights and hot, erotic thoughts.

He liked cool women, cool, calm, sophisticated women. Women who didn't provoke or challenge or arouse him to the point he couldn't think or sleep.

As she had tonight.

He'd been with Madeline for three years and yet he'd never

once lost sleep thinking of her. But tonight he felt absolutely obsessed with Hannah.

Thank God she'd be gone in the morning.

The sun poured through his office window, casting a glare on the computer screen, making his eyes burn.

Makin felt like hell.

It had been a rough night. A long night. He'd ended up going to bed just hours ago, and then sleeping badly, and now he was back at his desk at seven drinking cup after cup of coffee, hoping to wake up, gain some clarity and, with any luck, shake his sense of guilt and shame.

He'd treated Hannah badly last night and he was still angry with himself for losing control, for allowing lust and desire to cloud his thinking. He shouldn't have kissed her, shouldn't have reached for her, but that wasn't her fault. It was his.

He'd apologize to her later, just before he put her in the limousine on the way to the airstrip. And then he'd move forward. He wouldn't look back.

It was good. Everything was good. Hannah would be off after breakfast, his guests would arrive midafternoon, and he had sorted out his priorities.

Ringing for a fresh pot of coffee, Makin woke up his computer and checked the headlines of the various international papers for world news. He usually devoted an hour to reading his preferred papers every morning, and was reading the online version of *The New York Times* when he came across a link with the heading Argentine Polo Star in Fatal Crash.

Alejandro's accident had finally hit the newswire.

Curious to see if there was an update on Alejandro's condition, Makin clicked on the link and pulled up the article. He skimmed the piece but the article didn't cover anything new.

Makin looked at the three photos accompanying the story next. The first was one of Ibanez on his horse on the field, one posing with his team at the recent Palm Beach tournament, and one in which Alejandro was snapped talking with the Princess Emmeline of Brabant.

He ignored the first two photos, intrigued by the last. It was a recent photo, he saw, taken a week ago in Palm Beach at the polo tournament he'd hosted and Hannah had organized.

It wasn't the most flattering photo of either Ibanez or the princess, and Makin suspected they probably weren't even aware they were being photographed. Alejandro looked angry and the princess was in tears. It didn't require a lot of imagination to figure out what the fight was about. Perhaps the princess had discovered that there were other women? Women like Penelope. Women like Hannah.

Thinking about Hannah, Makin clicked on the photo, enlarging it. He felt a flicker of unease as he studied the princess.

She looked far too familiar, as if he knew her, but how could that be? He'd only been in the same room with Princess Emmeline once and yet looking at this picture, he felt as if he knew her... intimately.

Impossible.

He studied the photo intently, drawn by Emmeline's eyes and her expression.

He knew that expression. He knew those eyes.

His uneasiness increased.

He copied and pasted the photo onto his desktop and enlarged the picture once more, studying it carefully, analyzing the princess's slender frame, the tilt to her head, the twist of her lips.

She was clearly desperately unhappy. And while that wasn't his problem—the princess was most definitely not his problem—he recognized that face. It was the face he'd seen all night in his troubled dreams.

Hannah's.

A thought came, unbidden, and it made him even more uncomfortable than before.

Holding his breath, Makin opened the photo folder on his computer, pulled up the photo taken in Tokyo last year at a business dinner. It was a photo of Hannah accepting a ceremonial kimono. The shot had been taken at an angle, just like the photo of the princess talking to Ibanez. Hannah's hair had been pulled back in a low ponytail, much like the princess's chignon at the polo match.

He enlarged Hannah's photo and dragged it next to the shot of the princess.

The resemblance was uncanny. Their profiles were so similar. The chin, nose, brow. Even the eye color. Change the hair color, and they could be the same. Maybe identical. And to think they'd come so close to meeting each other in Palm Beach. They'd both been there at the polo field…they'd both attended Sunday…

Could they…could Hannah be…

No. No. It was too incredible, too impossible. People didn't switch places…that was a ludicrous idea, something that only happened in Hollywood movies.

And yet, when he glanced from the photo of Emmeline to the one of Hannah and back again, comparing the faces, the profiles, the lavender-blue eyes, he thought, *It could be done.*

Change the hair, swap the clothes, mask the accents and Hannah and the princess could easily pass for each other. Makin was rarely truly shocked by anything but he was blown away now. Dumbfounded, he crossed his arms over his chest and stared through narrowed eyes at the computer screen.

Why hadn't he seen it before? Why hadn't he picked up on the differences…the changes? Hannah's sudden extreme thinness. Her fragile beauty. The emotion in her eyes.

Hannah, the Hannah with him here in Raha right now, wasn't Hannah at all. She was Princess Emmeline d'Arcy, the twenty-five-year-old royal from Brabant engaged to King Zale Patek of Raguva.

Which meant he hadn't kissed Hannah, but Princess Emmeline.

It hadn't been Hannah who had captured his imagination and turned him on, it was Emmeline.

It was Emmeline he'd wanted. Emmeline who had created a night of hot, erotic thoughts.

Unbelievable.

He drummed his fingers on the desk.

Unthinkable.

He didn't know what game she was playing, but he'd soon find out.

Unforgivable.

He slapped his hand down hard on the desk and got to his feet. Time he paid a call on the princess.

CHAPTER SEVEN

EMMELINE answered the knock on her door, hoping against hope it was breakfast as she'd rung for eggs and toast a half hour ago, but it wasn't anyone from the kitchen on her doorstep. It was Makin Al-Koury, looking elegant and polished, if a tad forbidding in his black trousers and black shirt.

He must have just showered and shaved because his dark hair still gleamed, the skin on his bronze jaw was taut and smooth and she caught a whiff of his spicy sandalwood cologne. "You're up early," she said, her pulse racing, her stomach a knot of nerves.

"We're usually working by seven-thirty," he answered. "You've been taking it easy and sleeping in."

There was something rather chilling about his smile this morning and her heart faltered and plummeted, making a dramatic swan dive right to her feet.

Locking her knees, she forced herself to look up and meet his gaze head-on. His eyes were light and glacier-cool, like mist rising off ice.

Last night the kiss had felt so good, but now, in the clear light of day, she knew it had been a dreadful mistake. Sheikh Makin Al-Koury was too big, too powerful, and far from civilized. He might have millions and billions of euros, and expensive toys and homes scattered across the globe, but that didn't make him easy, or comfortable or approachable.

"No wonder you're sending me away. I've become unforgivably lazy," she answered lightly, forcing a smile as she placed an unsteady hand over the narrow waistband of her ivory lace skirt, hoping he'd be fooled by her bravado.

"No one can be perfect all the time." He smiled at her. "How are you this morning?"

"Good."

"And you slept well?"

He was still smiling but she felt far from easy. "Yes, thank you."

"Excellent." He paused, gazed down at her, his expression inscrutable. "In that case, I trust you feel well enough to take some dictation?"

"Dictation?" She hoped he didn't hear the slight stutter in her voice.

"I need a letter written, a letter that must go out today. I'm hoping to put it on the flight with you."

"Of course." Emmeline fought panic and reminded herself that she could do this. She could play the game a little longer…pretend a little longer… "Would you like me come to your office?"

"That's not necessary." He put a hand on the door and pushed it all the way open. "I'm already here."

Emmeline stepped aside to let him in. "I just need some paper and a pen."

"You'll find both in your desk in the bedroom," he said helpfully. "In case you've forgotten."

She darted a quick look into his face, trying to understand where he was going with this, because he was most definitely going somewhere and she didn't like it. "Thank you."

Heart hammering, stomach churning, she headed to the bedroom to retrieve the pad of paper and a pen from the desk, and then hesitated at the mirror hanging over the painted chest of drawers. She looked elegant this morning in her ivory silk blouse and matching lace skirt. She'd pulled her dark hair back and added a rope of pearls, and Emmeline could only pray that her polished exterior would hide her anxiety. She didn't know anything about taking dictation. She'd never dictated a letter, either, but she'd never let the sheikh know that.

Back in the living room, Emmeline sat down on the edge of the pale gold silk couch, pen poised. "I'm ready."

He glanced at her pen hovering above paper and then into her eyes. He smiled, again, all hard white teeth. "I'm not sure how to start the letter," he said. "Perhaps you can help me? It's for an acquaintance, King Zale Patek of Raguva. I'm not sure about the salutation. Would I say 'Dear Your Royal Highness'? Or just 'Your Highness'? What do you think?"

Emmeline's cheeks grew hot. She fought to keep her voice even. "I think either would work."

"Good enough." The sheikh sat down on the couch next to her, far too close to her. And then he turned so that he fully faced her. "How about we start with 'Your Royal Highness'?"

She swallowed, nodded and scribbled the words onto the top of the page before looking up at him.

"Something has come to my attention that cannot be ignored. It is an urgent personal matter, and I wouldn't bring it to you if it weren't important." He paused, looked over her shoulder to see what she'd written. "Good. You've almost got it all. And it's very nice handwriting, but I'd appreciate it if you took shorthand. It's hard to get my thoughts out when you're writing so slowly."

She nodded, staring blindly at the notepad, so hot and cold that she barely registered a word he said.

She couldn't do this. Heavens, how could she when she couldn't even breathe? Couldn't seem to get any air into her lungs at all. Was she having a panic attack? It had happened once before, on the night of her sixteenth birthday after her father had broken the news about her adoption.

She'd nearly collapsed that night as her throat had seized.

Her throat felt squeezed closed now. Her head spun. And it was all because Sheikh Al-Koury was sprawling on the couch next to her, taking up all the space, as he dictated a letter to her fiancé, King Patek.

A letter about an urgent personal matter.

Emmeline's head swam.

What could Makin Al-Koury possibly have to say to King Patek that was urgent or personal? If they were close friends, the sheikh wouldn't have her dictate a letter. He'd send Zale a text, or an email or pick up the phone and call. No, a formal letter was reserved for acquaintances. And bearing bad news.

"You missed a line," Sheik Al-Koury said, leaning close to point to the page. "The last thing I just said, about me discovering some disturbing information concerning his fiancée, Princess Emmeline d'Arcy. Write it down, please."

He waited while she slowly wrote each word.

"Your handwriting is getting smaller," he said. "Good thing I'll have you type it before sending. Now to continue. Where were we? Right, about his duplicitous fiancée, Princess—"

"I have that part," she interrupted huskily.

"Not duplicitous."

"You didn't say it the first time."

"I said it now. Put it in. It's important. He needs to know."

Her pen hovered over the page. She couldn't make it move. She couldn't do this anymore.

"Hannah," he said sharply. "Finish the letter."

She shook her head, bit her lip. "I can't."

"You must. It's vital I get this letter off. King Patek is a good person—a man of great integrity—and one of the few royals I truly like. He needs to be told, at the very least warned, that his fiancée can't be trusted. That she's unscrupulous and amoral and she'll bring nothing but shame—"

"If you'll excuse me," she choked, rising from the couch, eyes burning, stomach heaving. "I don't feel so well."

Emmeline raced to the bathroom, closed the door and sat down on the cold marble floor next to the deep tub. She felt so sick she wished she'd throw up.

Instead she heard Sheikh Al-Koury's words swirl and echo around in her head. *Duplicitous. Unscrupulous. Amoral.*

They would be her mother's words, too. There would be no one to take her side or speak up for her in defense. Her family would judge her and punish her just as they always had. Just as they always did.

The bathroom door softly opened and a shadow fell across the white marble floor. Jaw set defiantly, she glanced up at Makin as he filled the doorway, a silent challenge in her blue eyes.

Makin gazed down at the princess where she sat on the floor, a slender arm wrapped around her knees.

Considering her precarious situation, he would have thought she'd be timid or tearful, or pleading for forgiveness, but she was none of those things. Instead of meeting his gaze meekly, she stared him in the eye, her chin lifted rebelliously, her full lips stubbornly compressed.

One of his eyebrows lifted slightly. Was this how she intended to play it? As if he was the villain and she the victim?

How fascinating.

She was a far better actress than he'd given her credit for. Last night she'd moved him with her touching vulnerability. He, who felt so little real emotion, had felt so much for her. He'd wanted to strap on a sword and rush to her defense. He'd wanted to be a hero, wanted to provide her with the protection she so desperately seemed to need.

But it had all been an act. She wasn't Hannah, nor was she fragile, but a conniving, manipulative princess who cared for no one but herself.

The edge of his mouth curled. She hadn't changed. She was still the imperious, spoiled princess he'd met nine years ago at her sixteenth-birthday ball. He'd never forget that her father had thrown her a huge party, inviting everyone who was anyone, and she'd spent it throwing a tantrum, crying her way through the evening.

Embarrassed for her father and disgusted by her histrionics, Makin had left the ball early, vowing to avoid her in the future. And he had. Until now.

His narrowed gray eyes searched hers, thinking that in the past nine years little had changed. She still epitomized everything he despised in modern culture. The sense of entitlement. The fixation on celebrity. The worship of money. Skating through life on one's looks.

And yes, Emmeline was stunning—he wouldn't pretend that he hadn't wanted her last night—but now that he knew who he was dealing with, and *what* he was dealing with, his desire was gone. She left him cold.

Makin leaned against the white marble vanity, hands braced against the cool, smooth stone surface. He was furious and he needed answers, and he would have them now.

"You don't have the flu," he said shortly, his deep voice hard, the sharp tone echoing off all the polished stone.

She opened her mouth to protest and then thought better of it. "No."

"And you weren't sick yesterday because you had low blood sugar."

Her chin inched higher. "No."

Didn't she realize the game was up? Didn't she understand that he'd figured it out? That he knew who she was and that he was livid? That he was hanging on to his control by a thread?

Makin didn't speak, battling for that control, battling to maintain the upper hand on his temper when all he could see was red. "How far along are you?" he asked, when he could trust himself to speak.

Her eyes, those stunning lavender eyes, opened wide. They were Hannah's eyes, the same lavender-blue of periwinkles or rain-drenched violets, which made him suddenly hate her more. "The truth," he bit out.

She just stared at him, expression mutinous, lips firm. There was nothing weak or helpless about her now. Even sitting on the floor she looked regal and proud and ready to fight him tooth and nail.

How dare she? How dare she play the entitled princess here? Now? She should be begging for mercy, pleading for leniency.

"I'm waiting," he gritted impatiently, fully cognizant that if she were a man he wouldn't be using words right now, but his fists. Just who did she think she was, waltzing into his life as if she belonged here? He flashed to last night in the garden and how he'd reached for her, and kissed her, wanting her more than he'd ever wanted any woman. And it galled him—infuriated him— that she'd succeeded in making a fool of him in his own home.

"Seven weeks," she said at last, eyes darkening, the lavender-blue luminous against the pallor of her face. "Give or take a day."

Give or take a day, Makin silently repeated. God, he detested her. Detested everything about her, and everything she represented. "I take it Alejandro Ibanez is the father."

She nodded.

"And that's why you were at Mynt making a scene."

Her cheeks suddenly flushed, turning a delicate pink. "I didn't make a scene. He was making a scene—" She broke off, bit savagely into her lower lip and looked away, expression tortured.

For a moment, just a moment, Makin almost felt sorry for her. Almost, but not quite. "And my second question, Your Royal Highness, and an even more important question is, what have you done with my secretary, Hannah Smith?"

Emmeline's head jerked back around, her gaze wary as it met his. "What do you mean?"

For a moment he saw only red again, blazing-hot red, but then his vision cleared. "I'm not in the mood for games, princess."

"I...I don't know what you mean."

He was angry, so very, very angry, that he could have easily dragged her up from the floor and taught her a lesson. "You *know* what I mean."

"But I *am* Hannah."

Makin gritted his teeth so hard his jaw ached and his temple throbbed. "Don't insult my intelligence, Your Highness. You'll just make me angrier—"

"But I am—"

"—Emmeline d'Arcy, Princess of Brabant," he finished for her, his tone sharp and withering. "You've been masquerading as my secretary, Hannah Smith, for the past three days—maybe longer. That's the part you'll want to explain, starting right now."

"Sheikh Al-Koury—"

"How about we drop the titles? Cut out all the pretense of formality and suggestion of respect? You don't respect me, and I certainly don't respect you. So I'll call you Emmeline, and you can call me Makin, and, with any luck, I'll finally get the truth."

She slowly rose to her feet, smoothed her ivory skirt with the overlay of fine Belgian lace, which accentuated the rounded shape of her hips and the high, firm buttocks. Blood coursed through his veins. He suddenly felt hot and hard and even angrier.

How could he still want her? It boggled his mind that he could find her attractive now, after all of this....

"How did you find out?" she asked quietly.

"By chance." He looked down at her and his lips curled faintly, self-mockingly, even as his body ached with the need to take her, possess her. It wouldn't be gentle though. "I was reading *The New York Times* online, and came across a link to an article about Alejandro's accident. One of the photos accompanying the story was a shot of you and Alejandro talking at the polo tournament I hosted in Palm Beach."

"The only photo I took was with the Argentine team—"

"This wasn't a posed photo. It was candid. You were behind the stables and neither of you were happy. You looked as if maybe you were having a fight." He saw the light dawn in her eyes and realized he'd been right. They had been quarreling, and probably about the pregnancy. Of course Ibanez wouldn't want the child. He'd probably insisted she get an abortion, and for a moment Makin felt a flicker of pity for the princess but then squashed it. Emmeline d'Arcy deserved whatever she had coming. He wouldn't spare her a moment's concern.

"You were crying," he added flatly, harshly, refusing to let her get under his skin again, reminding himself that she was shallow and selfish and without one redeeming virtue. "That's when I knew." He paused, studied her pale face. "I knew that expression." *And I knew those eyes,* he silently added.

Now that he knew who was who, he could see how different Emmeline's eyes were from Hannah's. They might be the same shade, that astonishing lavender-blue, but the expression wasn't at all similar. Hannah's gaze was calm and steady, while Emmeline's was stormy and shadowed with emotion. If one didn't know better, one might think that Emmeline had grown up in a tough neighborhood, fighting for every scrap of kindness, instead of having lived an easy life in which luxury had been handed to her on a silver platter.

His chest grew tight. He told himself it was anger. But it wasn't just anger, it was betrayal.

He'd started to care for her, just a little. Just enough for him to feel used today. Played.

And no one played Makin.

"So what have you done with Hannah?" he asked, his tone icy with disdain. "I want her back. Immediately."

For a moment the princess didn't speak and then she took a deep breath, squared her shoulders. "She's in Raguva." She hesitated. "Pretending to be me."

"What?" Makin rarely raised his voice but it thundered through the marble bathroom.

She stood tall, appearing nonchalant, but then she ruined the effect by chewing nervously on her bottom lip. "I needed to speak with Alejandro about my pregnancy, but he wouldn't take my calls, not after that talk we had at the polo field following the tournament. I was desperate. I had to see him. I needed his help. So I begged Hannah to switch places with me for a day so I could go to him in person."

"And you couldn't go to him as yourself?"

"He was avoiding me, and even if he would see me, my staff and security detail wouldn't let me go. They'd been given orders by my parents to keep me away from him, and they were determined to follow those orders."

"Your parents were right not to trust you."

She shrugged, walked past him, leaving the bathroom. "Probably."

"Probably?" he demanded, following her. "Is that all you have to say?"

Her shoulders rolled, shrugging. "What do you want from me? An apology? Fine. I apologize."

Makin stood inside the bedroom doorway, astounded by her lack of concern. She was suddenly the epitome of calm and cool. How was such a thing possible? "When exactly did you switch places with my assistant?"

"Last Sunday. The twenty-second." She moved across the bedroom to enter the walk-in closet. She pulled an armful of clothes out and carried them to the bed.

She was packing.

She must assume that she was going somewhere.

"That was a week ago," he answered, leaning against the door frame, arms folded over his chest. Why pack now? Where did she think she was going? To London? On his plane? At his expense? How fascinating.

Emmeline nodded, emerging from the closet with a half dozen pairs of delicate high heels.

His brow lowered as he watched her place the shoes in tidy pairs on the bed next to her other garments. "And just how long were you planning on leaving my secretary in Raguva, Your *Highness?*"

Emmeline glanced up from the shoes, wincing at his sarcasm. He'd finally gotten to her. "I...I don't know," she confessed, sitting down on the edge of the bed next to her clothes and shoes. "I haven't figured that part out."

His gaze raked her up and down, expression merciless. "Unbelievable." His chest felt blisteringly hot while the rest of him remained cold.

She didn't answer. She didn't even try.

He took a step toward her, and then another, hands clenched at his sides. "Who do you think you are? How could you put my assistant in this position? Do you know what you've cost her?"

And still she said nothing.

"Her job." He was so angry, so very angry and yet Emmeline appeared remote, detached, as if she were above the fray. "She's gone. Fired. I've no need of her services anymore—not here with me, or in London, or back in Dallas, either. She's gone, finished, so be sure to give yourself a good pat on your back."

Emmeline's body jerked, shoulders twisting. "But you've made it clear that there was no one like Hannah—"

"There wasn't. But you changed that when you asked her to shift her loyalty from me to you—"

"She didn't. She hasn't!" Emmeline leaned urgently forward.

"She is still very loyal to you. Completely loyal. She loves working for you."

Finally, he thought. Finally some reaction. Some emotion. But it was too little, too late, for all of them. He shrugged indifferently. "Good. She's yours. She can now work for you."

"Please don't do that. Please. Hannah loves her job."

"Maybe she should have thought of that before she headed off to Raguva, pretending to be you." He started for the bedroom door, but paused to turn to look at the princess who still sat frozen on the edge of the bed. "And I'm not sure why you're packing. I don't know where you think you're going, or how you're getting there. Because you're in my desert, my world, princess, and you're stuck here with me."

And then he was gone, leaving the apartment with his emotions running high, temper hot, feeling even angrier and more punitive than he had an hour before.

There would be consequences. And she would not like them.

CHAPTER EIGHT

EMMELINE'S legs shook as the door closed behind Makin. She'd been shaking ever since he'd confronted her in the bathroom with the truth. Shaking with fear.

But now he was gone and she was glad. Glad he'd left her alone. Glad the truth was finally out. She'd hated lying to him. Hated pretending to be his perfect Hannah. And now she didn't have to lie anymore.

It was better now that he knew the truth. Even if it meant he'd never speak to her again. Better this way. Better to be honest about everything.

And he could say what he wanted about her. He could ridicule her and despise her, but she wouldn't give him the ability to hurt her anymore. Emmeline left the cool serenity of the white, apricot and gold bedroom for the garden.

She paced the private courtyard with the intensely sweet perfume of antique roses scenting the air as the hot yellow sun beat down, heating her skin. For many this palace would be a kind of paradise. But Emmeline had grown up in palaces surrounded by high stone walls and uniformed soldiers who changed position every four hours. She'd never been the tourist on the outside, admiring the pageantry and elegance. She'd been the captive royal inside the palace walls, locked in for her own protection.

And now, Kasbah Raha was just one more beautiful gilded cage.

One more luxurious but secure building to hold her, confine her, trap her.

And Makin was one more powerful man who thought he could intimidate her. Belittle her. Control her.

But she was done being manipulated and controlled. It was time she grew up. Wised up. Opened her eyes and used her brain. She had a good brain, too, and at twenty-five it was time she owned her life and made decisions for her future.

A future with a baby. *Her* baby. And how she loved her baby already. Her baby was the most important thing now.

"You look like a tiger in the zoo."

Emmeline jumped at the sound of Makin's deep voice and turned to see him inside the doorway, in the cool shadows of the air-conditioned living room. "So much for privacy," she said, folding her arms across her chest.

He shrugged. "You didn't answer the door."

"So you just let yourself in?"

"If I'm concerned about the safety of one of my guests."

"And so now you're concerned about me?"

He shrugged again. "I'm responsible for all the guests in my home."

The edge of her mouth curled up. "Did you forget something? Or have you thought of another way to humiliate me?"

"I don't have to, Your Highness. You do a great job of humiliating yourself." He gestured toward a bench in the dappled shade. "But I do have news. Sit."

She bristled inwardly at his sarcasm but refused to let him see how much he affected her. There was no reason for him to affect her. She told herself she didn't care for him. Certainly didn't need him. They were equals. And adversaries. "I'd rather stand."

"You're seven weeks pregnant. I'd rather you sit."

It was clear from the curt tone that he expected her to obey, but he forgot that he had no power over her. "You might, but I'd ask you to remember that I'm not Hannah—"

"Trust me, I do," he cut her off with a sigh. "So sit. There is something I must tell you, and it's not easy."

Emmeline's stomach fell and her knees went weak. Alarm shot through her. "Alejandro?" she whispered.

"Yes."

She put a hand to her belly, sixth sense telling her that Makin's news wasn't good.

Crossing to the marble bench in the dappled shade, Emmeline sat down, feeling the tug of the lace skirt around her hips and how her ivory silk blouse clung to her damp, warm skin.

"I'm sorry," he said simply.

Emmeline's heart sank into the pit of her stomach. "What happened?"

"He went into cardiac arrest a couple of hours ago. And even though they had the best doctors and nurses in all of Miami, they couldn't get his heart beating again."

It took her a second to process everything. "He's gone."

"Yes."

She closed her eyes, besieged by wildly different emotions. Shock, grief, regret. But the grief and sorrow weren't for herself, or Alejandro. They were for Alejandro's five children. Their lives would now be changed forever.

"Are you feeling faint?" Makin asked.

She shook her head, opened her eyes. "No."

"This must be quite a blow."

"Yes."

"I am sorry."

She pushed a loose tendril of hair back from her face. "You didn't like him."

"He was a father."

She nodded. "I feel for his children," she answered, realizing now that her child would never have the chance to know his or her father. "I wonder if they know yet. I wonder if his wife knows."

"Isn't that a bit hypocritical?"

"What?"

"To pretend you care about his family...?"

"Why shouldn't I?"

"You chase Ibanez, sleep with him—"

"I didn't know he was married until you told me, and I didn't chase him. He chased me."

"So that makes it okay to sleep with a married man?"

"No! Heavens, no! I'm horrified, disgusted. I made a terrible mistake."

"And your engagement? Did you not know about that, either?"

She swallowed around the thick lump filling her throat. No wonder Makin enjoyed ridiculing her. She sounded pathetic. Stupid beyond belief. "I did."

"That's a relief, because I'd hate to think that everyone but you knew."

She winced. Blood rushed to her cheeks again. "He pursued me, not the other way around. Some days he'd call or text over and over, and this went on for years."

"So you're saying it *is* okay to cheat?"

"*No*. But I wasn't married to Zale yet, and I was still hoping to marry for love, not money. My parents knew I didn't want an arranged marriage. I wanted a love match, and I thought since Alejandro loved me, we would have that."

"If you didn't want to marry Zale, why didn't you say no? Why enter the arrangement in the first place?"

Makin Al-Koury was a powerful man, and he understood a great deal about politics and economics. But he didn't know everything. He didn't know what it was like to be a woman. Much less a beautiful, sheltered young woman with no vocation, few practical skills and a numbing lack of real world experience. Emmeline's only purpose and power lay in her marriage ability. "Because I didn't have a choice."

"You were forced into the arrangement?"

She shrugged, worn out from trying to make him understand. He'd been raised by different parents, who had a different plan for him than hers had had for her. "There are different kinds of pressure. It's not always about physical force. Women can be intimidated emotionally, psychologically—" She broke off, shook her head. "But that's neither here nor there. The fact is, I have known since I was a little girl that my parents would choose my husband for me. They made sure that from a young age I knew my duty."

"Apparently they didn't. Because everyone but King Patek knows you've been hooking up with Ibanez over the years."

Emmeline flushed. "That's not true. We *never* hooked up."

"So you're not pregnant?"

"*Yes.* Yes, I did sleep with him. But it was only one time, and he was my...first." Her voice wobbled. "I was a virgin until then."

Makin snorted with derision.

Emmeline's flush deepened, heat spreading through her body until she tingled all over. "Believe what you want. I don't have to answer to you, or impress you, or try to make you like me. You and I will never see eye to eye—" She broke off abruptly and turned away, horrified to discover that she was about to cry.

Thank God he didn't say anything right away, or laugh. Thank God there was just the bubble and splash of the fountain. But the silence stretched too long. Emmeline glanced at Makin and saw his expression.

Hard. Unforgiving.

She swallowed around the lump in her throat and lifted her chin, refusing to be cowed by his judgment, knowing that others would look at her the exact same way. Including her parents. It would hurt. But it wouldn't kill her. Over time she'd learn to weather the disapproval without letting it get to her. She'd learn she could stand on her own two feet just fine.

"I know you don't think much of me," she said. "But I will be a good mother. I will do what's right for my child, starting with seeing a doctor as soon as I get back to Europe."

"Then let's stop wasting time and get you on a plane for Brabant—"

"I'm not going to Brabant. I'm going to London."

"Not back to Brabant?"

"No. Never."

"But that is your home, your country—"

"Not anymore."

"You can't change your birthright, Your Highness. You are descended from one of the oldest royal families in all of Europe. Your bloodline ties you to the very country."

"I will find a new country to call home. Lots of royals do it."

"Yes, in countries where monarchy has been replaced by democracy or socialism, but Brabant is still a constitutional monarchy and as far as I know, you are the rightful heir to the throne. Why would you give that up?"

"Because I'm not the rightful heir," she said huskily, walking away from him to approach the pool. "I'm not a true heir at all—"

"That's ridiculous."

She shrugged. "But true. And that's why I won't be going home, and why I won't be asking for forgiveness or mercy. I don't have to tell my parents anything. I'm twenty-five, of majority, and have access to the trust set up for me by my late grandfather. If I am careful, it's more than enough for me to live on."

"And your child?" he asked. "If you walk away from them, he or she may never be accepted by your family."

"I am sure he—or she—won't be," she said after a moment.

"Certainly not, if you plan on running away...hiding in the English countryside?"

"I wouldn't be hiding. I'd be living quietly, raising my child with, I hope, some privacy and dignity—"

"You hope?" His mouth tightened. "Is that your bright plan? To hope to have some privacy and dignity?" He made a rough, low sound of disgust. "Good luck, Your Highness. You're going to need it." With another low, derisive snort, he turned around and walked away.

She drew a quick breath, feeling as if he'd slapped her. "I might be running away but you're great at walking away," she called after him, hands curling into fists, her voice vibrating with emotion.

"What?"

"You can do it because you have power," she said as he turned to face her. "Most of us can't. We have to stand there and take it. But you don't have to. You're a man, and one of the world's richest. Everybody needs you. Everybody wants your approval or your protection. It must feel good."

He started back toward her. "How dare you speak to me in that tone of voice? You are a guest in my home. You are completely dependent on me—"

"I didn't ask to be."

"No, you didn't ask. You forced yourself on me by imperson-ating my assistant."

"Then let me go."

"I would love you to go."

She visibly flinched, stung. And yet, why did she care what he thought? Why did he have the power to hurt her? Swallowing hard, she walked around the pool and toward the house. "Great. That makes two of us. If you'll have a driver take me to the air-strip, I'll fly out immediately."

"With what plane?"

She stopped short. "The one you were going to send Hannah on."

"Oh, my plane. But that was for Hannah. You can send for your own."

"I don't have my own plane."

"I guess you'll need to ask your parents."

She clamped her jaw tight. "That's exactly what I meant when I said you love your power. You want the world to think you're this good, caring person. You put on conferences and host events and fund research, but you do it to prove you are superior."

"Someone should teach your some manners."

"It won't be you. You have none."

"Perhaps I should drop you off along the desert highway... see if any of my good Bedouin tribe members happen along and let you hitchhike a ride home. Or they may not. You might end up as desert road kill."

"What a gentleman."

"No. Wouldn't claim that one at all. But then, why do I need to be a gentleman? You're no lady."

"Having fun now, are you?"

A hot light flickered in his silver eyes. "No. Not at all. So help me understand what it is you want from me. Do you want pity? Sympathy? Poor Emmeline, poor little princess, she's been so mistreated—"

"Go to hell," she gritted, walking past him into the living room. He was so appallingly chauvinistic. So arrogant and self-righteous that she couldn't even believe this was the same man she'd kissed last night. And last night had been lovely. For a moment last night she'd felt something beautiful and good but all the goodness was gone, leaving her shaken and disillusioned.

"Where are you going?" Sheikh Al-Koury demanded, his sharp voice followed her into the living room.

"To finish packing. Your Bedouin tribesmen sound delightful compared to you."

CHAPTER NINE

WHEN Makin Al-Koury decided to act, he acted swiftly. And this time he'd acted so swiftly Emmeline's head still spun.

She couldn't quite believe she was seated on his jet as it taxied down the runway preparing for takeoff only thirty minutes after she'd told him his Bedouin tribesmen sounded delightful.

In retrospect, it probably wasn't the smartest thing to say. But then, Emmeline had struggled with containing her emotions ever since she was a child. One day she would learn control. One day she'd bite her tongue.

But until then, she'd suffer the consequences as she was suffering now.

Because she wasn't just flying to Brabant. She was being accompanied home by Sheikh Makin Al-Koury who had decided that she couldn't be trusted to make it home to see her parents. No, he'd decided to escort her all the way to the d'Arcy palace and leave her in her parents' care.

What a prince.

The jet was picking up speed, racing down the narrow black runway they'd landed on just twenty-four hours before.

It was déjà vu. Everything was as it had been—they were buckled into the very same seats they'd sat in on the way to Raha. She felt the same emotions, too. Anxiety. Dread. Fear of the unknown.

Emmeline felt Makin look at her as she choked on a gasp when the jet lifted off the ground in a dramatically steep ascent.

"Nervous flyer?" he asked.

"No." She forced herself to take a deep breath. She wasn't a nervous flyer, but she certainly hadn't expected to spend the rest of the day in Makin's company. It had been a tough morning and now it would be a very long day. "Just a little queasy from takeoff."

He hesitated, before asking gruffly, "Do you need anything?"

Her head snapped up in shock, lips parting slightly at his audacity. Did she *need* anything? Was he serious?

He was hauling her—by force—across the Middle East to Europe, to return her—against her will—to the royal palace in Brabant, and he wondered if she needed anything?

This. This was exactly what she didn't get. This is exactly what she didn't understand about him.

If he was so angry with her—and he was—then why did he care about how she felt? Why ask her about her comfort, or pretend to care about her well-being?

"Aren't your first guests arriving this afternoon?" she answered, suppressing her confusion, realizing she'd never understand him.

"Yes."

"You won't be there."

"I am fully aware of that."

"I thought this conference was so important to you."

"It is."

"Then shouldn't you be home, welcoming everyone, instead of flying twenty-nine hundred miles to haul me before my parents?"

"I thought it prudent to get you out of Raha before my guests arrived."

She saw his expression and understood. "You thought I'd be disruptive."

She saw that she'd hit the nail squarely on the head.

He didn't trust her. He thought she was a loose cannon, causing trouble wherever she went.

A weight settled in her chest, making it hard to breathe. He was no different than her parents. He looked at her and saw what he wanted to see instead of who she really was.

Chest tight, Emmeline glanced away, out the window at the

ea of gold sand below. *Let Makin think what he wants,* she told erself. *It doesn't matter...he doesn't matter...*

And yet in a small part of her heart, she could admit that maybe he did.

It had happened when he'd kissed her.

In Makin's arms she'd felt not just safe, but...desirable. Beautiful. And she never felt beautiful as a woman. She never felt like a real woman...and she hadn't, not until Makin kissed er, bringing someone to life inside of her.

The kiss had been the most amazing thing she'd ever felt. And he'd wanted more.

"I'm not dangerous," she said hoarsely, unable to hold the words in, or hide the hurt.

"You didn't say dangerous, you said disruptive."

"I wouldn't have embarrassed you."

"I couldn't have taken the chance."

"What about your guests? You're not even going to be there now to greet them as they arrive."

"My friend Sultan Nuri of Baraka has promised to do the honors."

Emmeline knew Malek Nuri, had seen him and his wife, the European princess Nicolette Ducasse, at a number of social events over the years. They were a gorgeous couple and so very happy together. "Does he know why you're not there? Does he know that you feel compelled personally to hand me over to the executioner?"

"You are so dramatic."

"So I've been told."

"As well as emotional."

Blood surged to her cheeks. "And you are so critical."

He studied her from beneath lowered lashes. "I hit a nerve, didn't I?"

"I've been criticized for being emotional my entire life."

Makin had been angry when they'd boarded the plane but now, seated across the aisle from Emmeline, he found it impossible to remain upset with her. He didn't know if it was because he bore such a strong resemblance to Hannah, or if it was because Emmeline was an enigma, but he was intrigued by her a▐ wanted to know more about her. "Who criticizes you?"

"My parents, particularly my mother."

"What's her complaint?"

"She has many." Emmeline wrinkled her nose. "But the ch▐ one seems to be my excessive emotion."

"Excessive...how?"

She ticked her mother's complaints off on her fingers. "I'▐ sensitive. I talk fast. I get nervous. I cry at the drop of a hat."

His lips twitched. "Do you cry at the drop of a hat?"

"Depends on the hat."

He grinned, amused, liking this Emmeline. She was unpr▐ tentious. Funny. Direct. "Have you and your mother always h▐ a strained relationship?"

"Since birth."

"Why?"

"I wish I knew."

She suddenly sounded very serious and his brow furrowe▐ She'd changed into jeans and a white peasant blouse before t▐ flight, and right now with her hair loose and no makeup, s▐ looked young and fresh. Appealing. Like the kind of girl you want to take home to meet your parents, and he suddenly wo▐ dered what his parents would have thought of Emmeline d'Ar▐ They'd known of her, of course, but due to his father's healt▐ they'd never met her.

"I was emotional as a boy," he said abruptly. "Sensitive. I never forget my mother pulling me aside when I was around eig▐ or nine and telling me I was a big boy now and too old to cry▐

"Do you remember why you cried?"

"My father had fallen out of his wheelchair. I was scared."

"But that would be frightening."

"I would see worse things."

"Sounds like you had to grow up at quite a young age."

He shrugged. "My mother needed me. It was important I strong for her, and my father."

Emmeline's expression was troubled and Makin realized t▐

nversation had become too personal. He swiftly changed the
bject to lighten the mood. "I've never seen you in jeans before."

Emmeline glanced down, crossed her legs, running a hand
er her thigh as she did so. "They're Hannah's. And Hannah's
. I found them buried in the back of her closet." She suddenly
ked at him. "I'm going to return them to her. I promise. I'll
ve them dry-cleaned and—"

"That's between you and Hannah. I imagine she's had to wear
ur clothes in Raguva. I can't picture her playing princess in
r wardrobe of brown, beige and gray."

Emmeline smiled crookedly. "She doesn't really have a cou-
e wardrobe."

"No. She's too practical for that."

Emmeline ran a hand over the worn denim again. "I've never
ned a pair of jeans like these. They aren't the designer ones.
ey're real. Broken in, so soft."

"Hannah was raised on her father's ranch in Texas, just out-
e of San Antonio. Has she told you some of her stories about
r life on the ranch?"

Emmeline shook her head.

"I think she found it lonely on the ranch. Her father raised
r. She didn't have a mother. She grew up riding and roping and
ping with roundups."

"Such a different life than mine."

"I can't see you on a ranch."

"Neither can I, but I do ride. Not Western-style, of course. I
ed to compete."

"Dressage?"

She grinned. "No, jumping. I was quite good." She must have
n the disbelief in his eyes because she laughed and added, "I
lly was. Even made the Brabant Olympic Equestrian team
twenty."

"You participated in the Olympics?"

"Well, I made it there, but ended up getting thrown in my
st event. It was a nasty fall, and for almost twenty-four hours
ad no feeling below my chest. Thank goodness full sensation

eventually returned, but that was the end of my riding. I'm
allowed to compete again."

"I had no idea."

"I can't imagine you reading tabloid magazines, so it's u
likely you'd know I was mad about jumping. It's not exac
mainstream news."

"Your accident would have made headlines."

"It was mentioned that I was thrown, but there was a ma
sive earthquake the next day, and the focus turned to real new

"How many years ago was that?"

"Five." She glanced down at her middle and pressed a ha
to the peasant blouse, flattening the cotton fabric over her st
flat stomach. "That's how I met Alejandro. He was at the cou
when I was thrown and he came to the hospital to check on m
The nurses wouldn't let him in. Alejandro being Alejandro-
She broke off, swallowed. "—he told them he was my fian
and they let him in."

Makin thought he'd known Princess Emmeline all of the
years. He thought he'd known everything important about her
beautiful, fashionable, chic, as well as soft, pampered and la
He'd imagined that her only ambition was being seen and ph
tographed. Instead she'd spent years training in a highly co
petitive, dangerous sport. She'd been thrown from a horse. S
was far stronger than he'd ever imagined.

"That's how the rumors and talk started," she added. "Ab
Alejandro and me. But we weren't involved. There was noth
between us, not until March."

"But over the years you were seen with him, time and aga

"Because he would search me out. Never the other way arou
I was never interested in him. He wasn't my type. I know y
don't believe me, but I worked very hard to rebuff him. Only
think that backfired. The more I pushed him away, the more
termined he was to win."

Looking at her stunning features—the high cheekbones,
angled jaw, the full mouth—he could believe it. She was beyo
beautiful. She had a rare, luminous quality, as though there v

ght inside of her making her shimmer and glow. "Men like
chase," he said.

"So I've learned." She tried to smile but it didn't reach her
s. "He didn't love me. He didn't even want me. He just wanted
.oh, what's that English expression? Score. He just wanted to
re." She met his gaze, smiled mockingly. "And he did. Now
s gone. I'm pregnant. And nothing will ever be the same,
l it?"

He felt such a sharp tug of emotion that it almost took his
ath away. She'd been through a difficult time and things
ren't going to be getting any easier. He suddenly knew she
ded a friend, someone in her corner. Someone who would be
re for her. "You're right. It won't be."

"I'm scared."

He felt another inexplicable tug on his emotions. Gone was
glossy, glamorous princess who had sailed through life un-
ched by the problems of ordinary mortals. She looked young
l real and heartbreakingly vulnerable. "You could end the
gnancy. No one would be the wiser."

"*I* would."

"It'd be the best thing for you."

"But not for the baby!" she flashed hotly, color suffusing her
eks. "And I know you don't like Alejandro—"

"This has nothing to do with him," he interrupted sternly.
nd I'm not a proponent of abortion. But I think you have to
very practical right now, think hard on your choices. You are
ncess Emmeline d'Arcy and the world holds you to a differ-
standard."

"Perhaps. But I could no more abort the pregnancy than am-
ate an arm or leg. I love this baby, and I want this baby and
prepared to make the necessary sacrifices to ensure that he
she has the best possible life."

Makin regarded her steadily, torn between admiration and
cern, aware that the road ahead of her would not be easy. But
wasn't about making the easy decision, it was about making
right decision, and if keeping the baby was the right thing for

her, then he supported her one hundred percent. Life was frag
and precious and full of unknowns.

Makin was all too familiar with the fragility of life. H
known since he was a teenager that he'd never be able to ha
children due to the gene he'd inherited from his father. And
at twenty, six months after his father's death, Makin had elec
to have a vasectomy to ensure that he couldn't carelessly or
cidentally impregnate his partner. He simply could not take
risk of passing on such a fatal, painful disease to his childr
It had been bad enough watching his father suffer. He could
imagine his own children suffering the same fate.

"Then you need to be strong," he said to Emmeline at leng
"You need to hold tightly to your convictions and do not let a
one sway you from what you believe is right and true."

They traveled in silence for nearly forty minutes and th
the captain announced that they would be starting their desc
momentarily.

Emmeline looked out the window and then at Makin. "We
still flying over desert."

"We're stopping in Nadir to refuel. We'll only be on
ground fifteen or twenty minutes." He paused, studied her bro
hair, aware that it wasn't her true color. "Do you have a perso
hair stylist?"

"Yes. She's in Raguva with Hannah."

"Which means she could be anywhere." He saw Emmelin
expression and clarified, "Hannah's no longer in Raguva. S
left the palace early this morning and should be on her way b:
to Dallas now."

"So King Patek knows?"

"He discovered the truth last night."

"My parents must know then, too."

"I did send word we were on the way and had to stop and
fuel. They aren't expecting us until midafternoon."

"It's going to be pretty ugly when we get to Brabant,"
said slowly.

"You have to face your family sooner or later."

"Then later seems preferable."

"Right now, maybe. But it's always better to confront problems ad-on. I act as soon as I can. It saves heartache down the road."

"That's why we're on the plane now. Better to get me home ickly than delay and risk more trouble."

"Exactly," he agreed, and then realized how it must sound her. He tried to soften the blow. "My father taught me not to eep things under the carpet or play ostrich by burying your ad in the sand. People will think you're ashamed or have some-ing to hide."

"But I do feel shame. I'm not proud to be a single, unwed other. I've made so many appearances trying to educate young rls, wanting them to be smart and careful, and yet I've failed do the very thing I preach."

"As you said, you made a mistake."

"A terribly stupid one."

Makin's insides tightened, his chest knotting with sensation, d he realized now it wasn't Hannah he'd wanted to send away sterday. It was this person, this woman. Emmeline. Not be-use he disliked her, or because she'd failed him in some way, t because she was making him care. Not about grand or im-rtant things like politics and economics, but about something ry small and personal. Her.

He did care for her. He was glad he was accompanying her me, if only to lend his moral support. "What's done is done," said. "You can't go back. All you can do is go forward."

"Yes."

"But I don't think you should go home like this." He indicated r hair. "Not as a brunette. Since your stylist isn't available, I ow someone who could help. She can meet us at the airport d board the plane when we refuel."

Emmeline touched her hair. "You're sure she'll come?"

"She's on my payroll."

"She's your stylist then?"

"No. She's Madeline's."

"Madeline?"

"My…mistress."

Emmeline frowned. "That's right. You mentioned her last

night." She hesitated. "Does Madeline mind that her stylist w
help with my hair?"

"I don't know." He shrugged, suddenly uncomfortable an
impatient. He wished he hadn't mentioned Madeline. There w
no need to bring her up, and he certainly had no desire to discu
her with the princess. "Risa is an expert at doing hair on this j
and she'll have you back to your natural color by the time v
arrive in Brabant."

Just a little over an hour later, they were back in the air after r
fueling in Nadir.

Risa, the hairstylist, had brought everything she might nee
in a large trunk. She had various boxes of color, foil square
cotton strips, shampoo and conditioner, as well as a hair drye
curling tongs, styling creams and finishing sprays.

On board, Risa immediately mixed color and applied it
Emmeline's hair, taking little strips here and there and wra
ping them in foil.

Now Emmeline sat on the bed flipping through one of th
magazines Risa had brought with her while she waited for th
color to finish processing, but her mind kept wandering fro
the magazine to Makin. Why did he have a mistress? What w
the point of a mistress? Why not a girlfriend...or a wife?

A knock sounded on the door. It was Makin. He opened t
door a crack. "Are you decent?"

"I'm dressed. But not sure how decent I look," she answere
setting the magazine aside.

He opened the door wider. "You look like an alien," he sai
taking in the pieces of foil and purple cream.

Emmeline smiled wryly. "You're not supposed to see th
part."

"Where's Risa?"

"In the galley kitchen rinsing the bowls and brushes
Emmeline closed the magazine and slid her legs off the be
"Risa's good, by the way. She knows what she's doing."

"She worked in Paris for ten years for a top salon befo
Madeline hired her away."

"Risa told me Madeline's blonde." Emmeline didn't know why she said it.

"She is," he agreed.

Emmeline waited for him to elaborate but he didn't. "Have you always had a mistress?"

Makin blinked. "What kind of question is that?"

"I'm curious. And you've asked me very personal things. I don't know why I'm not allowed to know anything about you."

"I never said you weren't."

"Good. So, why a mistress instead of a girlfriend? What's the point of having a mistress?"

He hesitated a moment than shrugged. "Convenience."

Her brows knit together. "For you?"

"Yes."

"And what's in it for her?"

"Comfort. Security."

"Financial security, you mean?"

"Yes."

"Because it doesn't sound as if there is emotional security."

"I wouldn't say that—"

"Because you have all the control. It's a relationship on your terms. You see her when you want, and she must be available whenever you call. Which, by the way, is horrible."

"Madeline's not unhappy."

"How do you know she's not unhappy?"

"Because she's never said she was."

"Maybe she's afraid to complain—"

"Madeline's not afraid of me."

"But she can't feel all that secure. She's not in a relationship with you—"

"Time to change the subject."

"Do you love her?"

"That's none of your business."

"Do you plan on marrying her?"

"Again, none of your business."

"But she's been your mistress for three years."

"Risa told you that, didn't she?"

"Don't blame her. I ask too many questions."

"I can believe that," he said dryly.

Emmeline flushed. "It's just that I would hate to be someone's mistress. I would hate to spend my life waiting for someone to call me or come see me."

"Madeline has friends in Nadir, and a busy social life attending parties and fashion shows."

"I'd rather be poor and have someone to love me, than to have lots of money and no love."

"You can say that because you wear couture and get invitations to the most exclusive parties—"

"But clothes and parties aren't real. Clothes and parties are frills…window dressing. I'd rather someone like me—want me—for me, than for what I have in a bank account."

Makin suddenly smiled and shook his head. "You're like a little dog with a bone. You're not going to drop it, are you?"

She looked at him for a long moment before smiling reluctantly. "I'm sorry. I guess I did get a little carried away."

"I admire your strong convictions."

Her smile stretched wider. "You know, you're not all bad, Sheikh Al-Koury. There are some good things about you."

"Just hours ago you were saying I was a power monger."

She blushed, not sure if she should laugh or cry. "Haven't forgotten. And I haven't forgotten that we're not friends. And that we don't like each other."

His lips curved faintly. "You're incorrigible. I don't think anyone could control you."

"Many have tried."

For a moment he just looked at her, his hard features set, his gray eyes narrowed. "You can't move to England. You'd be miserable."

"No."

"You would. You'd be living in a fishbowl. You couldn't go anywhere without a half dozen paparazzi following you."

"Not in the country."

"Most definitely. You are Princess Emmeline d'Arcy. Once the media discovers you are pregnant and single, you will never be left alone. The tabloids will haunt you. Photographers will shadow you. The paparazzi aren't going to disappear just because you want to live quietly."

"Well, I can't stay in Brabant, locked behind the palace gate, under my parents' thumb. It's not healthy."

"Don't you have a home of your own in Brabant?"

"My grandparents left me an estate in the north. It's quite pretty, a small castle with gorgeous grounds—orchards, a rose garden and even a small wood with a lake for fishing—but my parents have said that it'd cost too much for me to actually live there. Staffing it, running it, security. And so it's mine, but unlivable."

"I thought you said you had some money of your own now? That you'd come into your majority?"

"I do, but it's not enough to fund the running of a château, and my parents won't help cover the difference, nor will they ask the taxpayers to help. And I do agree with that. Our people don't need me being a burden. That's why I thought that I would just go somewhere else, like England, and find a small place that I could afford."

"I think your citizens would be hurt if you left them. They love you."

She thought of the large crowds that turned out every time she made an appearance, all ages, waving flags and carrying flowers, of all the little children who lifted their faces for a kiss. "And I love them. They have always been so very good to me. So loyal. But now I am pregnant, and it will bring them shame, which doesn't seem right. I was to have been their perfect princess, a replacement for my aunt Jacqueline who was a most beloved princess. She's been gone longer than she was alive, and yet they still mourn her."

"She was stunning."

"She was so young, too, when she died. Just twenty."

"But now you create a new life," he said firmly. "A new royal baby for your citizens to love and adore."

Emmeline throat ached with emotion. "But I'm not royal—"

"What?"

She nodded. "And Alejandro is a commoner so the baby won't be given a title, or be in line for the throne. That's how it works in Brabant." Her voice broke. "That's why I had to marry King Patek. I had to marry a royal, a blue blood. And obviously I can't marry Zale now—can't marry any royal—and so I'm no longer in line for succession. Which means, my child won't be, either."

"I don't understand. How can you not be royal? You are King William and Queen Claire's daughter—"

"*Adopted* daughter." Emmeline's eyes met his. She hesitated, struggling to find the right words when none of them felt good. "They adopted me when I was six days old. Apparently I'm a bastard, which even today brings Claire, my adoptive mother, endless shame."

He looked dumbstruck. "Do you know anything about your birth parents?"

"Only that my birth mother was a Brabant commoner. Young, pregnant and unwed."

"And your father?"

"No one knows anything about him."

"You can't find out?"

Emmeline shook her head. "It wasn't an open adoption. My birth mother had no idea who would be adopting me, and my parents are very private. I had no idea I was adopted until I was sixteen." She paused, tugged on the cuff of the blouse with unsteady fingers. "My father broke the news to me just before my birthday party."

Makin's eyes narrowed fractionally. "The actual day of your birthday?"

She shrugged. "I know it sounds childish, but it crushed me. I'd had no idea, and then suddenly my father was telling me I was illegitimate—a bastard—born of sin." Her lips twisted wryly. "There I was, in my beautiful party dress and brand-new high heels, my first real set of heels, feeling so grown-up and excited. Then Father called me aside and took it all away. I don't think he meant to hurt me as much as he did. But to call me a bastard? To tell his only daughter that she was a product of sin?"

Her smile slipped for a moment, revealing raw, naked pain. "I fell apart. I think I cried the rest of the night. Silly, I know."

"It would have been shocking for anyone."

"Maybe." She was silent a moment. "So you see, I understand the stigma and shame of being illegitimate. I know what it's like to be judged and rejected. Who knows who my birth parents were, or why they had to give me up for adoption? But they did; and they must have imagined it was the best thing for me. And maybe it was. But I do know this—I want my child—he or she is not a mistake. And I will do everything in my power to ensure that he or she has the best life possible."

CHAPTER TEN

EMMELINE sat on the edge of the bed while Risa blew-dry her hair with a big round brush, aware that once she was home, it would be absolute hell. Her mother would lose her temper, probably scream at her that she was stupid. Her father would look morose and deeply disappointed and let her mother do all the talking. It was how they handled problems. It was how they handled problems like her. Not that she'd ever done anything to be considered a problem before, but it was how they'd always viewed her.

Sometimes Emmeline thought she should do something outrageous to give them cause for complaint, as the worst thing she'd ever done—until now—was skinny-dipping while visiting her cousins in Spain. She'd been twelve and it had seemed so daring to swim naked at night in the palace pool. Thirteen-year-old Delfina had suggested it and ten-year-old Isabel had endorsed the idea so Emmeline, nervous and giggling, joined them. And it had been fun, up until the time the palace security reported them to their parents.

Aunt Astrid had given them a scolding but Emmeline's mother had been furious. She'd demanded to know whose idea it was, and when Delfina didn't speak up, Emmeline took the blame to protect her cousins.

Emmeline had expected that her mother would spank her and that would be the end of it. Instead her mother spanked her and sent her home to Brabant.

The spanking had been bad, but being sent away from her cousins in disgrace, so much worse.

In the fourteen years since then, not a lot had changed. Her parents were still distant, her mother rigid. Emmeline could only imagine their reaction to the news that she was pregnant. She was too old to be spanked or sent away, so what would they do this time? Lock her in a tower and throw away the key?

"Almost done," Risa said, turning off the blow-dryer.

Which meant they were almost there, Emmeline thought, hands knotting into fists.

While Risa was styling Emmeline's hair in the rear cabin, Makin sat in his seat in the main cabin replaying the last several conversations he'd had with Emmeline in his head.

She wasn't who he'd thought she was. She wasn't shallow, either. Just sheltered and naive.

How could you hate someone for being sheltered? Inexperienced?

He couldn't.

He understood now that she'd panicked back in March. She'd turned to Alejandro out of desperation, wanting someone to love her, knowing her prospective bridegroom didn't. She'd made a gross error of judgment, but she wasn't a terrible person. He couldn't condone her actions, but he couldn't dislike her anymore. Not when he understood how painful it had been for her to be married off to the highest bidder, as if she were an object instead of a smart, sensitive and shy young woman with hopes and dreams of her own.

Makin suddenly wished he hadn't been so quick to put Emmeline on the plane for Brabant. But it was too late to turn around. All he could do now was offer her his support and let her know she wasn't alone.

An hour later they were in the back of a limousine sailing toward the palace. Just before landing Emmeline changed into a black pencil skirt and a chic black satin blouse, which she accessorized with a long strand of ivory pearls. Her hair, now a gleaming golden blond, was drawn into an elegant chignon at the back of her head. She wore pearls at her ears.

She was nervous, beyond nervous, but she squashed every visible sign of fear, flattening all emotion, refusing to let herself think or feel. Things were what they were. What would happen would happen. She would survive.

"Not that it matters, but I'm not a fan of arranged marriages," Makin said abruptly, breaking the silence. "They're popular in my culture, but it's not for me."

She looked at him, surprised that he had shared something personal. "Your parents didn't try to arrange anything for you?"

He shook his head. "They were a love match. They wanted the same for me."

"Are they still alive?"

"No. They died quite a few years ago. My father first—I was twenty—and my mother the year after." He hesitated. "We expected my father's death. He had been ill for a long time. But my mother...she was still young. Just forty-one. It was quite a shock. I wasn't at all prepared to lose her."

"An accident?" she murmured.

"Heart attack..." His voice drifted off and he frowned, his strong brow creasing. "Personally, I think it was grief. She didn't want to be without my father."

Emmeline looked at Makin and the emotion darkening his eyes. Until he'd kissed her last night, she'd imagined him to be cool...cold...and quite detached. Now she was beginning to understand that with him, still waters ran deep. His cool exterior hid a passionate nature. "They were happy together?"

"Very. They had an extraordinary relationship, and they were devoted to each other, from the day they met until the very end. I was lucky to have parents who loved each other so much, and to be part of that circle of love. It made me who I am."

"So why haven't you married?" she asked, noting that he, too, had showered and dressed just before they landed. He now wore a gray shirt and black trousers, and the crisp starched shirt was open at the collar and exposed the hollow of his throat. His skin was the burnished gold of his desert, perfectly setting off his black hair and striking silver eyes.

And it was a good question, she thought, waiting for him to answer. He was gorgeous. Brilliant. Ridiculously wealthy. He would be the catch of the century.

His broad shoulders shifted. "I haven't met the right one."

"And what would she be like?"

"I don't know. I haven't met her yet. But I'll let you know the moment I do."

Makin saw her lips curve and her eyes dance as she laughed at him. He wouldn't have thought he'd like her laughing at him and yet he found himself amused by her amusement. She didn't laugh often, but now she came alive, mouth lifted, dimples flashing, light dancing in her eyes. She was joyous…mischievous…happier and younger than he'd ever seen her and it crossed his mind that he would do almost anything to see her smile like this again.

He glanced from her eyes to her appealing lips, and suddenly Makin wanted to touch her, kiss her, part those soft, full lips and taste her again as he had last night in the garden.

He'd thought it was the candlelight and moonlight and dark purple sky bewitching him, but now he knew better. He knew it was her. She was the magic. But he had Madeline, and Emmeline was pregnant. They each had their own path, a path they had been destined to travel.

"I have a plan," he said firmly, hating that his body had hardened and he felt hot and restless next to her. He couldn't let her affect him this way. He did have a plan—he had a vision—he'd vowed to do something significant with his life and he would.

If his father could be as successful as he had been with a disease so brutal and debilitating, a disease that destroyed his spine and his limbs, eventually robbing him of movement and speech, trapping his brilliant mind in a wasteland of a body, then Makin should be able to move mountains.

But he couldn't move mountains if he got distracted. One day he'd have time for more. But not now.

Not now, he repeated, his gaze moving to the pearls around her neck. He'd never been a fan of pearls. They reminded him too much of old ladies and uptight college girls in cashmere twinsets, but Emmeline made pearls look glamorous. No, make that sexy. The long strand around her neck hung between her breasts almost to her waist. They slid across the black satin of her blouse as she moved, outlining one soft swell of breast and then the other. He found it almost impossible to look away from the luminescent pearls.

He stifled a groan as he felt yet another hot surge of desire, his attraction to her now complicated by his desire to protect her. He didn't know when he'd begun to develop feelings for her, but he did care about her, and there was nothing simple about their relationship anymore.

"Not far now," Emmeline said quietly, the laughter gone from her voice.

The car was speeding from the freeway to a quiet city street, and she was focused on the old buildings passing by, but her expression was serene, her blue eyes clear and untroubled.

If one didn't know better you'd think she was heading to a fashion show and luncheon instead of an excruciating encounter with her parents.

If one didn't know, he silently repeated, realizing he'd never known her. Realizing he'd always looked at the externals—the impossibly beautiful young woman, her effortless style, her placid expression—and had imagined that she sailed through life unmarked, untouched, unconcerned with the human fray.

He'd been wrong.

Emmeline suddenly turned her head and looked at him. For a moment she just looked into his eyes, cool and composed, and then her lips slowly curved up. "Is there something on my face?" she asked, arching a winged eyebrow, looking every inch a princess. "Or perhaps something green in my teeth?"

He nearly smiled at the something green in her teeth. She was funny. All these years he'd thought he'd known her, but he hadn't. He'd known of her, and then he'd projected onto her, but he'd gotten her wrong.

She wasn't stiff and dramatic and petulant. She *was* emotional, but she was also smart, warm, with a mischievous streak running through her.

"I have a feeling you were a handful as a little girl," he said.

She wrinkled her nose. "I must have been. Until I was thirteen I thought my name was Emmeline-get-in-here-you're-in-trouble-d'Arcy."

Makin laughed softly, even as his chest suddenly ached. She *was* funny. And sweet. And really lovely. Heartbreakingly lovely and he didn't know why he'd never seen it before.

Was it because she was so pretty? Was it because she looked like a princess that he had assumed the worst?

"I'm glad I had the chance to spend the past few days with you," he said. "When you get past the body guards and ladies-in-waiting and multitude of assistants, you're quite likable."

She choked on a laugh. "Careful. Don't be too nice. I might think we were friends."

It crossed his mind that she could probably use a friend. He was beginning to understand there wasn't anyone in her life to protect her. It was wrong. "So tell me, how will it go once we reach your home?"

The warmth faded from her eyes. "It won't be pleasant. There will be hard things said, particularly from my mother."

"She has a temper?"

"She does. She can be…hurtful."

"Just remember, sticks and stones might break your bones…"

"…but words will never hurt me…" She finished the children's rhyme, and her voice trailed off. She smiled a little less steadily. "It'll be fine."

That smile nearly pushed him over the edge.

He understood then that it wasn't going to be fine. It wouldn't be fine at all.

He looked away again, out the window at the elegant gray eighteenth-century buildings lining the square. It was raining, just a light drizzle, but the gray clouds made the afternoon feel dark and gloomy. The only color on the streets were the rows of trees leading to the adjacent park, lushly green with new spring growth.

"It seems bad now," he said, aware that he was in danger of becoming too involved, caring too much. He needed to step back. Put some distance between him and Emmeline. He was merely bringing her home, returning her safely to her family. "But this will pass. In fact this time tomorrow you could have a whole new set of problems."

"Oh, I hope not," she answered with a cool, hollow laugh a
the palace gates loomed before them. "I think I have enough o
my plate. Don't you?"

Entering the palace salon where her parents waited was like walk
ing into a minefield, Emmeline thought several minutes later. She
hadn't even walked all the way through the salon doors before
her mother exploded in anger.

"What were you thinking? Were you even thinking?" Queen
Claire d'Arcy was on her feet in an instant, her voice a sharp ric-
ochet of sound. "Or was your intention to humiliate us?"

"Absolutely not," Emmeline answered firmly, forcing her
self to keep putting one foot in front of the other, closing the gap
between them. In a dim part of her brain she knew that Makir
was behind her but he was the least of her worries now. "I would
never want to humiliate you—"

"But you did! Zale Patek didn't give us a specific reason why
he felt it necessary to break off the engagement, only that he
was concerned about a lack of compatibility. *Compatibility*," the
queen repeated bitterly. "What does that even mean?"

"He was merely being polite. The fault is mine."

"Why am I not surprised?"

Emmeline ignored the jab. "I'm sorry to have disappointed
you—"

"When haven't you?"

"—and will try to make amends."

"Good. At least we agree on something. You are to return to
Raguva immediately and beg His Highness for forgiveness. Do
whatever it is you must do, but do not return without his ring on
your finger—"

"I can't."

"Emmeline, it's not an option. It's your duty to marry him.
Your duty to provide heirs for him—"

"I can't, Mother. I'm already pregnant."

The grand salon, coolly elegant in white and gold, went
strangely silent. For a moment there was no sound, no motion,
and then her mother sank into her chair by her father's side.

Finally her mother's head tipped. "What did you just say, mmeline?"

Emmeline glanced at her father, who, so far, hadn't said a ord. True to form he sat silent and grim, letting her mother do ll the talking. "I...I'm..." She drew a deep breath. "...nearly ight weeks pregnant."

"Please tell me I heard you wrong." Her mother's voice ropped to a whisper.

"I wish I could." Emmeline's voice sounded faint to her own ars.

"And of course it's not Zale Patek's."

"No."

"Slut."

Emmeline heard Makin hiss a breath, but she didn't even linch. She'd expected this. Had known it wouldn't be pleasant. And it wasn't.

"How dare you?" Claire choked on the words. "You ungrate-ul girl! How dare you throw every good thing we have done for ou back in our faces?"

Emmeline felt rather than heard Makin move to her side. "I'm orry," she said quietly.

"That's it? That's all you have to say for yourself? You ruin our chances, you ruin us, and you're *sorry?*"

Emmeline lifted her chin, determined to stay calm, deter-mined to remain strong. Tears would serve no purpose, just make her look weak and emotional. Instead she'd accept the conse-quences, no matter how painful. It'd been her decision to sleep with Alejandro. Now she had to deal with the repercussions. "Yes. And while this is the last thing I wanted to happen, it has, and I'm going to take responsibility."

"And may I ask who the father is? Or is that secret knowl-edge?"

Emmeline's lips parted but Makin spoke first.

"I am," he said clearly, his deep voice firm.

Emmeline turned to face him, jaw dropping in shock, but he didn't even look at her. He was staring straight at her mother, a

snarl twisting his lips. "I am," he repeated fiercely, "and I wou
like a little bit of respect, please."

Emmeline's legs turned to jelly, even as her head spun. Sh
reached for Makin. "What are you doing?" she choked, as h
fingers curled around hers.

"Making this right," he growled.

She shook her head frantically. "It won't…it won't, trust me

"No. It's time you trusted me." And then with a small, ha
smile in her parents' direction, he walked Emmeline out an
closed the doors behind him.

In the hall Emmeline's legs threatened to give out. "Do yo
have any idea what you just did?" she said, holding his ar
tightly.

"Yes." He frowned at her. "You're feeling faint, aren't you?

"A little."

He swore beneath his breath and swung her into his arms. '
should not have brought you back!"

"But you did. Now, put me down. I'll be fine in a moment.'

He ignored her, exiting the hall for the grand foyer with th
blue-painted dome, and began to climb the stairs two at a time

"Makin, please. I can walk."

"Not going to have you faint and risk having you, or the bab
hurt," he answered, continuing up the marble steps with single
minded focus. "Isn't your room up here somewhere?"

"On the second floor, yes. But I won't faint—"

"Good." He shifted her weight in his arms as he reached th
top stair. "Right or left?"

She peeked over his shoulder, saw the familiar hall witl
ivory-painted woodwork, gleaming chandeliers overhead an
the pale gold-and-ivory carpet runner underfoot. "Right. But
can walk—"

"Fantastic. Which room?"

"That one," she said, nodding at a closed door. "And yo
didn't need to claim the baby. I was going to tell them the truth.'

"The truth?" he repeated, leaning down to turn the knob an
push the door open, giving her a whiff of his subtle spicy cologne
the scent that always made her insides curl.

"Yes," she answered breathlessly, growing warm and warmer. It's what you told me to do."

"Until I saw your mother in action and thought she was the evil."

"Makin."

"I did. I still do." He crossed the bedroom floor with the same long strides that had eaten up the stairs and hall. "No wonder Alejandro seemed like an attractive option. Your mother is terrifying!"

"She didn't terrify you."

His arms tightened around her. "No. But she did make me angry."

Emmeline inhaled sharply as he held her even closer to his chest. His body was muscular and hard. His spicy fragrance eased her senses and she could feel his heart thudding beneath her ear. Alejandro had been cold in bed. She didn't think Makin would be cold. She didn't think he'd be detached or indifferent, either.

The thought of Makin in bed with her, naked next to her, was both thrilling and terrifying. He was beyond gorgeous, but too big...too strong...too overwhelming in every way.

She was glad when he placed her on the bed and she scooted to the middle to try to clear her head.

He gazed down at her, his arms crossing over his chest, emphasizing the width of his rib cage. "You're an adult, Emmeline. You don't owe them your soul."

"My mother thinks I do."

"I noticed." He shook his head in disgust. "That's why I spoke up. She wanted a name, so I gave her one."

"But that's just going to make things worse, Makin. She's going to expect you to provide for the baby—"

"I will."

"No, you won't. It's my baby and I'm responsible. Not you."

His strong jaw firmed in protest, and she didn't think he'd ever looked quite so powerful and primitive and male.

"And so what do you want me to do, Emmeline? Just leave you here with them? Allow your parents to ride roughshod over you?"

"I can manage them."

"Just like you did in the salon?"

Heat rushed to her cheeks and she jerked her chin up. "I wasn't that bad."

"Have you lost your mind? That was horrendous. A blood bath. If it had been your father speaking I probably would have punched him."

"Makin!"

"I'm serious."

"I appreciate your support, I do, but telling them you're the baby's father isn't the way. We have to go tell them the truth before it's too late." Her voice broke and a tendril of pale hair slipped from her chignon to tumble against her cheek. "And please understand that while I appreciate you speaking up for me, it's time I stood on my own two feet—"

"So what do you want me to do?" he interrupted. "Stand by and do nothing? Allow your mother to attack you? Destroy you?"

Her heart suddenly ached. Hot tears filled her eyes. "Sticks and stones, Makin, remember?"

He held her gaze for an endless span of time. "But the rhyme has it wrong. Words can hurt. They were crushing you."

For a second she couldn't breathe: her chest on fire, her heart in pain. "She doesn't really mean it," she whispered. "It sounds worse than it is. Mother just has a temper."

"She crossed the line, Emmeline. She said too much."

"She did. But she'll calm down and feel bad later. She eventually always apologizes.'"

"That doesn't make it right."

Her shoulders twisted. "I know. But this is how it's always been and I'm not going to change her now."

"So what do you want me to do?"

"Go back to Kadar. Focus on your conference. It's an important conference for you."

"But you're important, too."

Her lips twisted wryly. "Not as important as all those dignitaries gathered at Kasbah Raha."

His light eyes searched hers. "I won't let them hurt you anymore, Emmeline."

"They won't. The worst is over."

His jaw flexed, a muscle popping, tightening near his ear. "You're sure of that?"

She suppressed all thought but freeing him. This wasn't his mess, or his mistake, and she couldn't let her life take over his. "Yes." She held out her hand to him. "And I hope we can part as friends."

His hand slowly enveloped hers, his gaze holding hers captive. "Friends," he repeated slowly.

She nodded, forcing a smile to her lips to hide her sudden rush of emotion. She would miss him. She'd grown to like him. Probably far more than she should. "Can we stay in touch? Maybe we could drop each other a line now and then?"

"That sounds like a plan."

CHAPTER ELEVEN

AFTER Makin left, Emmeline stayed in her room and even took dinner there, unable to face anyone.

She wished Makin had stayed.

Not because she needed him to fight her fights, but because he was good company. Interesting company. And he made her feel interesting, too.

She liked that he listened to her when she talked, liked how his eyes rested on her mouth, his brow furrowed intently. No one had ever talked to her as much as Makin had. No one had ever cared so much, either.

She fell asleep missing him, and woke up thinking of him and was grateful when her father sent for her during her morning coffee, if only to get her mind off Makin.

Emmeline's hands shook as she finished buttoning her navy silk blouse. She'd paired it with a long skirt the same color and added a wide, dark chocolate crocodile belt at her waist that matched her high heels. It was a mature, elegant, subdued look, perfect for the morning after yesterday's histrionics.

She slipped a necklace of Murano glass beads around her neck, the beads a swirl of gold, bronze and blue, and wondered if her mother would be waiting in the library or if this was to be just a father-daughter talk. One of those unbearably tense conversations her father had with her, where he talked and talked, and she listened and listened?

Regardless, she had to go. Dressed, with her hair drawn back into a smooth ponytail, and just mascara on her lashes, she left her room for the library, each step making her stomach churn.

Makin must be back in Kadar now, surrounded by his beloved desert and his important work. She felt an ache in her chest, near her heart.

Emmeline knocked firmly on the library door and waited for King William to permit her to enter. When he did, she found him seated at his enormous desk searching for an item in the center drawer.

"I had no idea," he said, frowning into his open drawer as she crossed the room to stand before his desk. "I wish you had spoken up."

She folded her hands in front of her, her own brow furrowing; she wasn't at all sure what he was referring to but she knew better than to interrupt.

"It would have helped if you'd explained, might have made the scene in the salon less uncomfortable." He looked up at her now, blue gaze reproving. "It was damn uncomfortable. Especially with Al-Koury there."

She sucked in a breath, hating the butterflies she got every time Makin's name was mentioned. "Yes, Father."

"But at the same time, I understand why you didn't say anything. I understand that Al-Koury wanted to speak to me first, and I appreciate the courtesy. I'm glad he's a gentleman and wanted to ask for your hand properly—"

"What?"

"Although to be quite honest," he continued, "Al-Koury should have come on his own, asked for your hand, before traveling with you. It is irregular, what with you being engaged to Zale Patek. A bit presumptuous. Put me in the hot seat, especially with your mother. But you're both human. Things happen."

"Father," she said sharply.

But he wasn't listening to her. He never did. His shoulders rolled as he just kept talking. "But it's not quite so easy for your mother. She's struggling to take it all in as she's very traditional and hasn't adapted to the way young people do things today. In her mind, you don't get pregnant and then married. You marry and then have the baby."

Emmeline blinked at him. Her father was speaking French but it could have been Mandarin or Egyptian. Because what he was saying didn't make sense at all.

King William lifted a hand. "But I promised Al-Koury we wouldn't criticize you, and we won't. I also promised that we'd focus on the positives, and so let me congratulate you. Al-Koury will be a good husband. And you know I like Patek, I do. But Sheikh Al-Koury...he's big money. Serious money. One hundred billion, two hundred billion, maybe more—"

"Father!"

"You're right. I shouldn't mention his wealth. But it is important, and he and I are to sit down later and discuss the pre-nup. You had quite a contract with Zale Patek. I'll negotiate just as hard for you with Al-Koury."

"Father."

"Yes, Emmeline?"

"I don't understand."

"Don't worry about the pre-nup. That's between him and me. And the lawyers, of course. His are flying in as we speak." He paused, looked at her for a moment and then smiled. "Your mother wouldn't approve of me saying this, but she's not here. I'm proud of you, Em. To snare one of the world's richest men. That says something. He's not an easy man to please and it's obvious he dotes on you. Congratulations, my dear. You did very well."

"When did you speak with him?" she asked, her voice strangled.

"Last night. After you'd gone to rest. He came to see me."

"He said he was going home," she whispered.

"Maybe to his room. We gave him the Ducalle Suite. I personally thought we could have done better but your mother isn't entirely happy about a sheikh for a son-in-law, but she'll come round. She always does."

"He's still here?"

"Of course."

She swallowed hard. "Father, there's been a mistake."

He closed the drawer hard. The entire desk rattled. "How so?"

"We're not...we're not...engaged."

"Well, you weren't. Not until Makin asked for your hand, and I've given him permission to marry you. I'm sure he'll give you the ring today—"

"Father, he doesn't love me. He barely likes me."

His eyes rolled. "Certainly liked you enough to get you pregnant."

"But Father—"

She was drowned out by the shrill ring of the telephone on his desk. It was a large antique phone and took up an entire corner of the table.

"I've said all I intended to say," he said, raising his voice to be heard over the ring. "The sheikh will be asking for your hand this morning. He'll put a ring on your finger and your mother should be calm soon. Now I must take this call—"

"He's not the father. It's not his child."

"Emmeline, I can't hear you over the phone. Please, go. I'll see you tonight at seven. We're meeting for drinks and then a celebratory dinner. See you then."

In the hallway, Emmeline put her hands on her hips and took a deep breath and then another, trying to process everything her father had said.

Makin hadn't gone home? He'd stayed and spoken with her father? He'd asked for her hand in marriage?

What was the sheikh thinking?

Wishing she'd had more than coffee and a roll for breakfast, Emmeline set off for the Ducalle Suite but Makin didn't answer the door. She knocked a second time, harder.

A maid popped her head out of a room from across the hall. "Sheikh Al-Koury is downstairs, Your Highness. He's having coffee on the terrace."

Emmeline grimly thanked her and headed for the large terrace where she found Makin at a table outside enjoying breakfast in the morning sun.

"What have you done?" she demanded, voice shaking as she

marched toward him. She'd missed him this morning and had wanted to see him, but not on these terms.

"Sorted things out," he answered calmly, stirring a half teaspoon of sugar into his coffee. "Made things right."

"No! You didn't make things right, Makin. You made things worse."

"How so?"

"My father is in the library rubbing his hands gleefully, anticipating getting his hands on some of your money, which won't ever happen as we're not getting married."

"I told him we are."

"Apparently you did. But you didn't ask me—"

"I didn't, no, not yet. But you need to be protected, and by marrying me, you will be protected—"

"How arrogant."

"But true."

"But I won't marry you. I don't want to marry you."

"Why not?"

Her eyebrows arched. "You need reasons?"

"Yes."

She shook her head, incredulous. "You're arrogant, controlling, and you keep mistresses."

"I've already ended my relationship with Madeline."

"You're mad!"

"Don't be shortsighted. This is the best thing for the baby, and in your heart you know it."

"It might be the best thing for the baby, but it's not the best thing for me."

"Why not?"

"I didn't want this kind of marriage. If I'd wanted an arranged marriage I would have married Zale. But I didn't. And I don't need you and my father making bargains in his library."

"You are being dramatic."

"Maybe I am," she choked, pulling out a chair across from him and sitting down heavily. "But you know we're not suitable. You know we're not compatible and you only asked for my hand because my mother was screaming."

"She does have a loud voice."

"See?" Emmeline was near tears. "You asked my father for my hand because you hate excessive emotion, and weren't comfortable with the shouting and crying, and so, to keep from feeling powerless, you took control the only way you knew how."

He sipped his coffee and returned the cup to the saucer. "Is that how it was?"

"Yes."

"Interesting, but not true. It *was* a scene in the salon yesterday, and your mother showed a side of her personality that I've never seen before, and hope to never see again, but Emmeline, you're mistaken if you thought I felt powerless. I knew exactly what I was doing."

For a moment she couldn't think of a single thing to say. *"What?"*

"I knew what I was doing when I left your bedroom. I fully intended to speak for you."

"But you did it out of pity," she whispered, suddenly chilled. "You did it because you couldn't bear not to do anything."

He looked at her long and hard, his dense black lashes concealing his expression. "You still have it wrong. I didn't do it because I couldn't bear not to do anything. I did it because I could do something. And I wanted to do something."

"But how does it help?"

"Because it changes everything. It gives your baby a name and a family. By marrying me, your child will have legitimacy, security and respect. He or she will want for nothing."

"Except your love."

"You can't say that. You don't know that."

"But I *do.* I was a baby adopted by well-meaning people, and they gave me every material thing they could, but it was never enough. I never felt wanted. I never felt loved. And I won't do that to my child. Not ever!"

Emmeline didn't wait for him to respond. She turned and practically ran, dashing down the terrace steps to the stretch of emerald lawn. She hurried across the lawn, her high heels sinking into the grass with every step, her emotions wildly chaotic.

When she turned and disappeared around a tall yew hedge, the grass gave way to gravel and the path led to the rose garden and Emmeline let out a hiccup of sound.

She hated him, hated him, hated him!

How could he do this to her? She'd trusted him. Trusted him to protect her.

Emmeline blinked back tears and walked in circles around the rose garden, but her quick steps failed to soothe her. Her emotions ran even hotter.

She felt betrayed by Makin. Worse, she knew he was right.

Marrying him would change everything.

Marrying him guaranteed her child a life of unknown luxury and protection. There would be private jets and private schools and round-the-clock security. The baby would be envied, admired, doted on by all simply because he or she was Sheikh Al-Koury's child.

Amazing what money and power could do.

And she'd be a fool to walk away from that kind of power and security just because she wanted more. Because she needed love.

Emmeline swallowed hard, torn between the knowledge that Makin could provide a good life for her child and the desire to be free and independent, aware that freedom and independence would come with a price.

People would talk. People could be cruel. People could make her baby's life a living hell.

Emmeline paused, her gaze skimming the rosebushes. It was too early and cool yet for the roses to be in bloom and they still looked sharp and thorny, still shorn from the pruning they'd had several months before. She felt like the rosebushes—bare, prickly, unlovable.

"I'm not King William." Makin's deep voice came from behind her, at the entrance to the rose garden, and he sounded furious. "Nor am I Queen Claire. I am Makin Tahnoon Al-Koury, and I am here because I choose to be here. I didn't have to fly to Brabant with you. I could have put you on the plane and sent you off. But I didn't. I wanted to travel to the palace with you. I wanted to be there when you announced you were pregnant—"

"You wanted to see me humiliated?"

"No. I wanted to make sure you were all right. And when I listened to your mother tear you apart yesterday, I realized you needed me. You needed someone to stand up to her and tell her to back off. You needed someone to believe in you. Someone to protect you. And I can. And I will."

"But why? You might be altruistic when it comes to third-world nations, but you've no patience with spoiled, cosseted, self-indulgent royals like me."

"Obviously, I didn't know you. I thought I did, but I was wrong. But now that I do know you, there's so much to like—"

"Like, not love. You don't love me. You don't. And you can't pretend you do."

His silver-gray gaze raked over her, from the top of her pale golden head to the tips of her dark heels. "I don't have to love you to want you." He paused to allow his words to register, his expression intense. "And I do."

She stared at him, her heart starting to race. "You mean… my body."

"I mean you."

"But you don't want *me*."

His lips curved, his expression dark and dangerous. "Oh, but I do," he said, closing the distance between them and drawing her toward him.

She stiffened as she came into contact with the hard heat of his body, and she flashed to the kiss in the garden in Raha. The kiss had been lovely and yet overwhelming—hot, intense, beautiful, but it had made her want and need. She couldn't let herself go there again. Couldn't risk letting her heart hope again. "No," she choked, trying to twist free.

His head dipped, his mouth slanting across hers, silencing her protest.

It wasn't a light kiss or a tentative kiss. Makin kissed her hard, his lips parting hers with ruthless intent. She shuddered as his tongue plundered her mouth, taking and tasting her as if she already belonged to him.

But she didn't. She belonged to no one and she struggled to

free herself, but he was too strong. She couldn't escape. Panic flooded her. She wouldn't be bought and sold. Wouldn't be handed over from one man to another. She wouldn't go through life spineless and powerless.

Furious, she bit Makin in the lower lip.

He cursed and lifted his head, arms loosening around her. His eyes glowed like molten silver. "What was that for?"

She punched him in the arm. "You don't own me!"

"Of course I don't. You're a woman, not a piece of property."

"Then why make a deal with my father before you come to me?"

"Because I was trying to help you—"

"You're just like him. Just like all of them. You don't respect me. You don't respect women—"

"Absolutely not true," he snapped, cutting her short. "I admired my mother immensely. She handled complex, difficult situations with dignity and grace, and I respect her more than anyone else I've ever met."

"What did she do that made her so admirable?"

"What didn't she do? She was a modern European woman married to a sheikh in the Middle East. She had to cope with my father's illness. She modeled strength and courage for me. And most of all, she was loving. She loved my father." He hesitated, shrugged. "She loved me."

"And that makes her remarkable."

"Yes."

He said it with such conviction and authority that she immediately believed it. And the fight suddenly left her.

Emmeline exhaled in a hard whoosh of air. "But you work so hard to accomplish things…"

"I do. But that's because there isn't a lot I need for me. I'm financially solvent. I'm blessed with good health. I've always felt loved and wanted. And so I can afford to focus on others, which allows me to give back."

"And so there's nothing you want? Nothing you need?"

"I didn't say that. Because I do want something. I want you."

His deep voice sent a thrill through her. *I want you.* There wa such authority and purpose in his voice. Such firm conviction that she felt another ripple of shock and pleasure.

Alejandro had said he'd wanted her, but he'd always been the charming playboy, handsome but flirty and playful. Makin Al-Koury was far from flirty and playful. Makin was fierce and powerful and supremely focused. When he said he wanted her, she felt it in her bones.

"But why me?"

He was silent a long moment, his features hard, lashes lowered over his intense gaze. "You have no idea of your worth, do you?"

"I'm an expensive headache, Sheikh Al-Koury. A constant problem requiring attention." She smiled and yet her eyes burned.

"Everyone needs attention. And princesses—particularly beautiful princesses—are notoriously expensive."

She laughed, and his gaze dropped to her mouth as if he found it absolutely fascinating.

"I did some research on your riding career last night after you'd gone to bed," he added.

"Did you?"

He nodded. "Even watched several videos of you competing. You were extraordinary, Emmeline. Does your family have any idea of how gifted you are?"

She shifted uncomfortably. "I'm not that gifted. When I finally made the Olympic team I fell—"

"Listen to yourself. You *made* the Olympic team." His voice dropped, deepened. "You *made* the Olympic team. And I repeated that for your benefit because your family seems to have done nothing but break you down when they should have built you up and given you confidence and support and unconditional love."

Emmeline had to look away, absolutely overwhelmed by the fierceness in Makin's voice. She knew him well enough to know he meant every word he was saying. He truly believed she deserved support and love…unconditional love…and it staggered her. Made her ache for all the things she'd never known and made her hope for all the things she still wanted.

Love. Security.

Happiness.

After a moment when she was sure she had her emotions firmly in control she looked up into Makin's face, studied his lip. "Did I hurt you?"

He licked the inside of his lip. "Just a little blood. Nothing serious."

"I drew blood?"

"You have a mean bite."

She knew he was teasing her but she felt bad. "I'm sorry."

"I'm fine. And I'm glad you got mad. I'm glad you have some fight in you. Life isn't easy and one can't just lie down and die when things get hard."

"Is that what you would teach the baby?"

"Absolutely."

"Even if she's a girl?"

"Especially if she's a girl. Life's difficult and you're going to be confronted by adversity, and you're going to get knocked down. But that's just part of life and so you get up and shake yourself off and keep going."

"I thought only weak people got knocked down."

"Everybody gets knocked down. The secret is the getting up again. That's why I value mental toughness—resilience. You don't want difficulties to break you. You want them to make you stronger."

She was silent as she processed this. "Marrying you is definitely the right thing for the baby, but it's not easy for me. I have a lot of pride. I don't like being dependent on others. I don't want others to come in and fix my mistakes, or sort out my problems for me. That's my job. I'm not helpless or stupid—"

"Good. Because I'd never marry a woman who was."

Emmeline looked at him a long moment, her pride warring with common sense. Marrying him would be the best thing for the baby. It would give her child a home, a name, legitimacy. And yet it wasn't that simple. Emmeline had hopes and dreams... there were things she'd wanted for herself. Like marrying the man she loved.

"It would be so easy to just give in, Makin, and let you be Prince Charming and allow you to sweep me off my feet and right all the wrongs…but that's not what I want from a man. Not anymore."

"What do you want?"

"To be the prince. To wear a sword and ride off on the white stallion and slay my own dragons." She laughed at the picture he'd painted, but it was true. She was tired of being helpless and broken. Tired of needing fixing. "There is a strong person inside of me. I just have to find her. Free her."

"I think you're on your way," he answered, taking her hand and slipping his fingers through hers.

Makin's hand was warm, strong, and she glanced down at their entwined fingers, at the gold of his skin against the pale ivory of hers. It felt good to hold his hand. She felt good with him at her side. Maybe one day she could be a woman like Hannah or his mother. Maybe one day he could respect her…maybe even love her. "Did you really end things with Madeline?"

"Yes."

"Why?"

"Because when I marry you tomorrow I am forsaking all others."

"You mean that?"

"Of course."

"So…our marriage…will be real?"

"Absolutely."

"Oh."

"You look shocked."

"Not shocked. Just nervous."

He led her to the bench near the sundial, and sat down, and drew her onto his lap. Emmeline blushed as she felt the warmth of him through his trousers, and the corded muscles of his thighs against her backside, and shifted uneasily. "Why nervous?" he asked, running a hand over her ponytail.

She liked the feel of his hand on her hair. It felt good. Warm. Soothing. As well as a little sexy. "I…don't have a lot of expe-ience."

"You said Alejandro was your first."

"Yes. And it wasn't good. I didn't like it."

He shifted her around to look into her face. "The first time isn't usually the best."

"I don't think I'd enjoy it after thirty times with him. It just wasn't...good."

"Did you like kissing him?"

She shook her head. "It didn't feel like anything."

"Did you like kissing me?"

Heat surged to her cheeks. She looked away. "It was all right," she admitted grudgingly.

"Just all right?"

She glanced back at him. His lips were twitching. He was trying not to laugh. "Are you fishing for compliments?"

"No."

"Sounds like it."

"No, I'm quite confident in that department—"

"Maybe a little too confident."

"You think so?"

"Quite possibly."

"Let's test that theory, shall we?" he asked, dipping his head his mouth slanting across hers.

As Makin's head dropped, he breathed in her fragrance—fresh light, sweet—and he hardened instantly. But he kissed her slowly this morning, taking his time, aware that he had all the time in the world because she would be his. She'd be his wife. His lover. The mother of his child. Call it fate or karma, but she was meant to be his, and now he kissed her as if it was the first time and he was just discovering the shape of her lips, and the softness of her mouth.

He felt Emmeline tremble against him, leaning toward him and he held her closer, but even then, he refused to rush.

Maybe one day she could be a knight or brave prince, but she wasn't there yet. She didn't believe in herself yet. Didn't even know who she was yet.

Right now Princess Emmeline reminded him of Sleeping Beauty. She needed to be woken with a kiss, a proper kiss, a kiss that would let her know she was beautiful and desirable and safe

He'd never hurt her. He'd always protect her. She needed to know that first. And then she needed to know how much he wanted her.

Because he did.

He slid the tip of his tongue along her upper lip, finding nerves in the delicate skin, and felt her nipples harden against his chest. His tongue flicked the other lip and he heard the hitch in her breath.

She was growing warm and pliant against him, her body molding to his, and it took all his self-control not to unbutton her blouse or pull up her skirt to get at her bare skin. He wanted to feel the seductive softness of her skin, and explore her tempting curves. He ached to have her naked and wet and open, but he'd make sure she was ready. Not just physically, but emotionally.

Emmeline's first time had hurt her. Her second time needed to be perfect.

Reluctantly he lifted his head. He gazed down into her eyes. They were darker now, deep purple, and cloudy with passion. "Marry me, Emmeline."

"And what do you get out of this, Makin?"

His lips brushed hers, sending an electric shiver dancing up and down her spine. "You."

CHAPTER TWELVE

THEY were supposed to be having a pre-dinner cocktail with her parents that evening in the elegant wood-paneled chamber her father favored, but her mother hadn't yet appeared.

Emmeline was sitting on the narrow loveseat with Makin at her side but she couldn't get comfortable, not when his thigh pressed to hers.

He was warm and making her warmer. And she couldn't relax. Her thoughts were absolutely chaotic and running wild at the moment.

But then, they had been all day, ever since she'd woken up and discovered that Makin had asked her father for her hand.

Which made no sense. At all.

Why would Makin do that? He said he wanted her. But that made no sense, either.

It really didn't.

Emmeline shot Makin a mistrustful glance from beneath her lashes. He was big, powerful, wealthy, gorgeous…he could have anyone…and he said he wanted her?

No. Impossible. Her father had to be paying him something. But Makin was one of the richest men in the world. He didn't need money…

"If your father wasn't here, I'd kiss that look off your face," Makin growled at her, his voice pitched so low only she could hear him.

Emmeline cradled her glass of ice water closer to her stom-

ach and hissed, "Stop acting like a caveman. I'm not something
you can just tackle and drag next to the fire."

"No? I quite like the idea."

She cast him another reproving glance. He didn't quell in
the slightest, but then, Makin was tall, strong, thickly muscled.
"You're unbearable. Now please scoot over. You're crowding me."
Which was true. They were smashed together on this tiny settee
as if they really were a newly engaged couple. *A couple in love.*

He was a horrible man.

A horribly confident and terribly appealing man.

She wondered yet again what he'd be like in bed.

Emmeline's insides suddenly flipped, her breath catching in
her throat, her breasts exquisitely sensitive.

"It's called cozy, Emmie."

"Well, I don't like it." Because sitting this close to him, she
couldn't see, hear, feel or think of anything but him. And the
way he kissed. And how his hands felt on her. And how she felt
when he was holding her…

She liked it when he held her. Liked his mouth on hers, and
her body against his and she'd never felt this way about anyone before. She'd never wanted anyone before and she wanted
Makin. But she wanted more than just lips and hands and skin.
She wanted all of him.

Which was so confusing…

"I didn't pick this room, or the couch," he retorted.

True. This was the room reserved for close friends and family, and despite the high ceiling and tall windows framed in rich
dark green velvet curtains, the chamber was filled with petite
antique pieces that had been passed down for generations. Pieces
that had been made hundreds of years ago for people who were
definitely smaller than they were today.

"I wonder what's keeping your mother," her father said with
a frown. "Perhaps I should go check on her?"

"I can go, if you'd like?" Emmeline offered, seeing an opportunity to escape.

"No need for you to race around in your condition," William

answered, setting his drink on an end table. "You stay and relax. I'll enquire after your mother."

Makin glanced down at her as the door closed behind her father, a lazy smile playing at his lips. "Nice try."

She stood up, walked away from him. "This is all so...fake."

"How so?"

"Our engagement—"

"No, that's real. I asked for your hand in marriage, and we are getting married tomorrow." He paused. "By the way, you look incredible." His voice deepened with appreciation, his gaze slowly drifting over her bared shoulder to the pink-and-plum shirred fabric shaping her breasts and outlining her flat tummy, before falling to a long train of pale pink at her feet. "I don't think I've ever seen you look better."

She glanced down at the asymmetrical neckline of her dress and then lower, to where the plum color gave way to the pink over her hips. It was a very slim, very body-conscious evening gown and in another month or two she'd start to show and she wouldn't be able to wear it. "It's the dress," she said, touching the bodice covered in crystals. "Couture does that for a woman."

"It's the other way around, Emmeline. You make the dress." He held his hand out to her. "I have something for you."

She shivered as she glanced at him where he sat on the small antique couch. He was huge and the couch was tiny and she could still remember the way it had felt to sit so close, the heat of his hip warming her, the corded muscle of his thigh pressing against hers. "You make me so nervous, Makin."

"Why?"

"I don't know. But every time I look at you, I get butterflies."

"Then I'll come to you." He left the couch, walked toward her and, removing a ring box, he snapped it open.

Emmeline blinked at the enormous diamond ring cradled by the darkest blue velvet.

"Give me your hand," he said.

Her fingers curled into a fist. She couldn't take her eyes off the ring. The diamond was huge. Four carats? Five? "Is that what I think it is?" she whispered, mouth drying.

"Yes."

"I can't wear that."

"Why not?"

"It's ridiculous, Makin. Far too extravagant. Something small and sentimental would have been nice—"

"It's my mother's wedding ring."

"Oh." She exhaled in a whoosh, and looked up at him apologetically. "I'm sorry. I didn't mean it that way—"

"You jump to conclusions too quickly."

Her heart was racing now. She felt almost sick. "I know. Another fault of mine," she murmured, putting her left hand in his. She was shaking as he slid the ring onto her finger. The stone was an immense princess-cut diamond, and smaller diamonds crusted the narrow band.

The ring was stunning. It glinted and sparkled as it caught the light.

Tahnoon Al-Koury had given this ring to Yvette, Makin's mother. Makin now gave it to her. Her heart suddenly ached. "It's really lovely," she said huskily.

"And so are you."

Her head lifted. Tears shimmered in her eyes. "I'm not. Not really."

"How can you say that, Emmeline?"

"Because I'm not."

"Have you looked in a mirror?"

"Yes."

"And what do you see?"

"Faults, flaws—" She broke off, bit hard into her bottom lip. "Makin, I'm not the woman in the magazines. I'm not that beautiful, glossy princess."

"Thank God."

Her head jerked up. Her eyes met his.

"I don't want a wife who is beautiful but fake, Emmeline. I want someone real. And you, Emmeline, are real."

He was prevented from saying more by the arrival of her parents. Her mother led them to dinner in the Crimson Dining Room. The table, of course, was impossibly elegant, with the royal china being used on top of heavy silver chargers. Crystal glittered beneath the antique chandeliers and dinner was subdued, conversation stilted, for the first half hour of the meal. But the wine was flowing freely, and as the second course was removed, Queen Claire became livelier.

Emmeline glanced nervously at her mother, aware that alcohol always made Emmeline's father quieter and her mother more chatty. Claire was becoming extremely chatty—practically verbose.

Makin was still on his first glass of wine and Emmeline wondered what he was thinking.

Makin caught her glance and smiled at her, which made her stomach do a funny nosedive.

He was really too good-looking. Feeling jittery and shy, she glanced down at her left hand resting in her lap to study the enormous engagement ring. It was the whitest stone she'd ever seen, and the exquisite cut continued to catch the light, glinting bits of blue, white and silver fire.

She glanced at him again and discovered he was looking at her, his silver-gray gaze intense.

Tomorrow night at this time they'd be married. Husband and wife. And from what he'd said earlier, he intended to be a real husband to her....

"Don't say I didn't warn you," Claire repeated, gesturing for one of the footmen to fill her wineglass again. "She's always been a problem. From the time she was an infant. There has never been a baby that cried so much."

Emmeline felt Makin's gaze on her again, but this time she looked pointedly away, a small, tight smile on her face. She wasn't a problem. She didn't know why her mother always seemed to think she was. It's not as if Claire had ever taken time to know her. They were rarely alone together. Her parents had busy, important lives and Emmeline had been raised by hired help—nannies and tutors—before being sent to a very small private girls' boarding school in France not long after she turned fourteen.

The boarding school had a reputation for being strict, but Emmeline had been happy there. There was order to the day and the rules were logical and consequences appropriate to the crime. Emmeline didn't mind that fraternizing with boys was absolutely forbidden.

School was the place she could escape her mother's unsmiling gaze and the tension that permeated the d'Arcy family palace.

"You can't really blame her, Claire, she was quite small at birth," her father interjected, rousing himself from his usual silence. He glanced at Makin, brow furrowing, bushy gray eyebrows pulling together. "She was not even four pounds when we got her. I think the nanny tried five different formulas before we found one she could tolerate."

"See? Emmeline has always been impossible to please," Claire added thickly. "Even as an infant, she had a temper. She'd cry for hours. Refused to be comforted."

"Babies cry," William said.

Emmeline glanced at her father, surprised that he was defending her. He rarely took on her mother, but perhaps the wine tonight had given him liquid courage.

William's expression softened as he gazed at her. "You look lovely tonight, Emmie."

She was touched by the compliment. Her lips curved in a smile. "Thank you. It's the dress—"

"It's not the dress," William interrupted. "It's you. You've grown up and you are…you look…just like her."

"Who, Father?"

"William!" Claire rebuked.

But William lifted a hand as if telling his wife to be quiet. "Your…mother."

"I'm her mother," Claire corrected stiffly.

"Birth mother," William amended.

Goose bumps covered Emmeline's arms and the fine hair at her nape stood on end. Stunned, she glanced at Claire and then back to her father. "Did you know my birth mother?"

"Yes," her father answered after the faintest hesitation. "And we think, in light of tomorrow's ceremony, you should know who she was, too."

Emmeline's pulse raced. Her hands shook in her lap. "Who

was she? What was she like? Did you ever meet her?" The questions tumbled from her as fast as she could say them.

"Of course we met her," Queen Claire answered brusquely. "We wouldn't adopt just any baby. We couldn't raise just any child. We adopted you because you were…different."

"Different?" Emmeline repeated wonderingly.

Claire took a sip of wine. "Special," she added coolly. "You weren't just any baby. You were royal."

A moment ago Emmeline's heart had raced. Now her blood seemed to freeze in her veins. *"Royal?"*

"Your mother was Princess Jacqueline," her father said, getting to his feet. "My sister."

Emmeline shook her head. "No…I don't…no…"

"It's true," Claire said flatly, slurring a little as she stared into her now-empty wineglass with some consternation. "William's baby sister. You were, what? Ten years older than her?"

He stood next to the table, fingertips pressed to the cloth. "Twelve." He sounded grave. "She wasn't planned. My parents had given up on having another. She was quite a surprise." His voice suddenly quavered. "My parents adored her. I did, too. No one imagined that by sending her away…no one could have dreamed…it was a mistake, a terrible, terrible mistake."

Emmeline's head spun. "I don't understand. My aunt Jacqueline died at twenty from a rare heart condition—"

"That was a fabricated story her parents told the public to cover the sordid facts of Jacqueline's death," Claire said with great relish. "Your mother died giving birth to you. Now you know the truth."

For a moment all was silent and then Emmeline spoke. "All these years you've known, but you hid the truth from me. Why?"

"It didn't seem relevant," Claire answered.

Emmeline exhaled in a rush. "Perhaps not to you, but it's everything to me."

Claire banged her hand on the table. "And why is it so important?"

"Because."

"That's it?"

"Yes." Emmeline rose, stood for a moment with her fingertips pressed to the table. "It's how I feel. And I have a right to feel what I feel. I have a right to be who I want to be. I think I'm going to have coffee and dessert later. If you'll excuse me."

She turned now to Makin and offered him a devastating smile. "Would you care to join me, darling?"

Makin would never forget that moment. He would have clapped if it had been appropriate. It wasn't.

But this…this was why he wanted her. This was why she was his.

She was brilliant. Stunning. Majestic.

He'd listened to the revelation regarding her birth mother in silence, disgusted that William and Claire had kept the truth from her and even more disgusted that tonight's dinner was when they'd chosen to share the news.

But they had. And Emmeline had handled it with grace, strength, dignity.

He loved her for it.

She was every inch the royal d'Arcy princess. Daughter of Europe's beloved Princess Jacqueline d'Arcy.

Jacqueline would have been proud.

He rose to his feet, buttoned his black dinner jacket. "Yes," he said simply, firmly, and offered her his arm.

Emmeline's legs felt like jelly as they exited to the hall and she was grateful for Makin's arm. Grateful for his support.

Her legs continued to feel like jelly as she climbed the stairs to her room and she held his arm tightly, thinking she couldn't have gotten through this without him.

He gave her confidence. He made her feel safe. Strong. Good. As if she truly mattered.

And somehow, with him, she almost believed she did.

Emmeline swallowed hard as they approached her room. "Never a dull moment around here, is there?"

"No," he agreed, opening the door for her and then following her inside.

She wandered around the room for a moment, too agitated to sit.

She wasn't the daughter of a Brabant commoner. Her mother had been Princess Jacqueline, Europe's most beautiful royal, and she'd died in childbirth. She'd died giving life to her.

It was terrible. Tragic. But at least Emmeline now knew the truth.

"So now you know," Makin said quietly, arms folded across his chest. "It was a horrible way to find out, but at least you know. There are no more secrets. No more skeletons in the closet. It's all out in the open."

Emmeline turned, looked at him. "If she hadn't had me, she'd be alive."

"If her parents hadn't sent her away to give birth in secret, she would have lived."

"You think so?"

"Yes."

She nodded, and rubbed her arms. "And here I am, twenty-five years later, single and pregnant, too."

"Yes. But things happen, mistakes happen, and we learn from them. We grow from them. And I look forward to starting a family with you. I think it's going to be quite interesting."

Her lips curved in a tremulous smile. "It certainly will be a change."

"And an adventure." He smiled back at her. "You're good for me, you know. You're shaking things up. Making me feel alive."

"And you give me confidence. I'm already stronger because of you."

"You were always strong. You just didn't know it."

"I wish it were true."

"It's true." He closed the distance between them, and took her hands in his, kissing one palm and then the other, and finally her mouth.

He was just deepening the kiss when her bedroom door opened and a muffled cough came from the hall.

Makin lifted his head and, blushing, Emmeline faced her father who was standing in the hall holding an enormous garment bag. "It wasn't all the way shut," William said gruffly. "I can come back later."

"No," Emmeline said, cheeks still hot. "Come in, please."

William hesitated. "I don't know if this will fit, but it was Jacqueline's. She wore this gown for her debutante ball. Mother saved it, and I thought perhaps you might want to wear it for the wedding...." His voice drifted off. He swallowed uncomfortably. "You might already have something—"

"I'd love to wear it," Emmeline interrupted him, taking the garment bag from him. It was surprisingly heavy. Must have a huge skirt. "But you didn't have to bring it here yourself. You could have sent it with one of the maids in the morning."

"I know. Claire said the same thing, but I wanted to see you. To make sure you were okay."

"Come in," she repeated, carrying the garment bag to the bed.

"I shall go," Makin said, "and let you two talk." He dropped another kiss on Emmeline's lips before walking out, closing the door quietly behind him.

William stood in the middle of the room, hands in his pockets. "My timing is terrible."

"I'm glad you're here. There are so many things I'd like to know."

"I imagine there are." He hesitated. "I know it sounds cruel, what my parents did, sending Jacqueline away to give birth. But they were old-fashioned, and they'd been raised in a time where unplanned pregnancies were hushed. Covered up. They thought they were doing the right thing. They truly believed they were protecting Jacqueline. They had no idea it would turn out the way it did."

"I don't remember my grandparents as cruel," she said, sitting down on the bed next to the garment bag.

"They weren't," he agreed. "And losing Jacqueline destroyed them. She was their baby. They never recovered from her death. After the funeral, Father moved to the dowager's château on the edge of the city, and Mother remained here to be close to you."

"Did Grandmother spend time with me?" Emmeline asked.

"She did. In the beginning. She was with you almost every day. Claire had to fight her for you. They had terrible rows—" He broke off, laughed as he sat down heavily, but the laugh sounded like pain. "I'm so sorry. Emmeline, we got it all wrong. We just tried to protect Jacquie, and then you, and it didn't work. The truth is so much better. Remember that."

She nodded, thinking that this was the time to tell him. He'd opened the door for her, created trust. Now all she had to do was tell the truth and confess that Makin wasn't her baby's father, that Alejandro Ibanez was, tell him that with Alejandro gone, Makin had offered for her out of some misguided sense of duty.

She knew her father would free her of the engagement. He couldn't possibly insist on her marrying Makin once he knew the truth.

But before she could find the right words to break the news, William reached for her hand and he carried it to his cheek. "You don't know how happy I am for you." He squeezed her fingers, overcome by gratitude. "It means so much to me that you have what your mother never had. The opportunity to marry the man you love, to have a normal life...or as normal as you can as a princess."

Emmeline's throat sealed closed as she watched the emotions—pain, relief, hope—pass one by one over his lined face. He'd had a far harder life than she'd ever imagined. "It's difficult to have a normal life when you're a royal, isn't it?" she said to him.

"It is. Especially when you're as beautiful as you are." He kissed her forehead. "I'm glad you have Makin. He's not the sort to indulge in make-believe. You can rest assured he's marrying you for all the right reasons. Now get some sleep, my dear. Good night."

CHAPTER THIRTEEN

MAKIN watched Emmeline walk down the palace chapel on her father's arm. King William wore his black royal uniform, a military dress coat from when he'd served in the Brabant Air Force as a twenty-year-old. His posture was as erect and proud as if he were still a military man.

But it was Emmeline who held Makin's attention, Emmeline who took his breath away in her mother's white debutante gown with a tiara on top of her golden head.

More ivory than ice-white, the strapless, heart-shaped bodice hugged her breasts and rib cage before nipping in dramatically at Emmeline's small waist. The very full silk skirt was covered in a pleated swirling pattern made to look like overblown roses, with the beaded ivory silk flowers growing larger as they moved toward the hem. The skirt's pleated silk caught the light and created shadows. Makin didn't think she could have picked a more beautiful gown to be married in.

For Emmeline, the brief wedding ceremony passed in a blur of sound and motion. There was the sound of the organ playing something too loud and bright. She and her father walked down the chapel aisle, the pews empty except for her mother in the front and the bishop waiting at the altar with Makin.

She felt her father kiss her and then give her hand to Makin. She heard the bishop's voice, and then heard Makin saying words, repeating the vows. She repeated the same vows. The bishop spoke again and then there was the exchange of rings. Makin lifted her veil and kissed her on the lips.

And it was done.

They were married.

There was an even briefer gathering after, consisting of wedding cake and champagne. Emmeline had a sip of champagne and a couple of bites of cake but couldn't eat or drink more than that.

She caught a glimpse of her reflection in the Gold Drawing Room mirror, seeing the swish of her full silk skirt from the back and the small, corseted waist. The dress hadn't needed to be altered a bit. It fitted Emmeline perfectly, which meant she and her mother had been the same size. Small. Slender. Elegant.

Emmeline suddenly wanted out of the dress, away from Brabant. This was the old life. She was ready for the next.

"Have you had enough cake and champagne?" she asked Makin.

His gaze held hers a moment, the silver depths warm. "Yes."

"I have, too. I'm going to go change."

"I'll call my flight crew, let them know we'll soon be on the way."

Upstairs, Emmeline had nearly finished changing into traveling clothes—a trim designer suit in taupe and pink. She'd just slid her heels on and was putting in the first of her pearl earrings when her bedroom door opened and closed.

Emmeline turned around to find her mother standing awkwardly by the door. "I came to offer my help, but you've already changed," Claire said crisply.

"Yes," Emmeline agreed, attaching the other earring. "Everything's packed. Just need to switch out my purse and I'm ready to go."

"Have you rung for someone to take your bags?"

"The maid did."

"Do you need…any money, or anything…before you go?"

Emmeline's lips curved but the rest of her face felt hard. "No. Makin's loaded. He'll take care of everything."

"Emmeline!"

Emmeline's eyes burned, and she swallowed with effort, her throat aching with suppressed emotion. "What do you expect me to say, Mother? Two days ago you made it perfectly clear how you felt about me. That I was an embarrassment, a problem, nothing short of a failure—"

"I never called you a failure!"

"But an embarrassment and a problem."

The queen took a slow breath. "You haven't been an easy child."

"But I'm not a child, Mother. I'm twenty-five…a woman who is going to have a child, and I can promise you this, I will never tell my child that he or she is a problem or an embarrassment. What a horrible thing for a mother to say to her daughter."

"I was caught off guard."

"Apparently you're always caught off guard."

Silence descended in the room, twilight casting long shadows across the bedroom floor, turning the rose-patterned carpet into shades of lavender and gray.

Claire cleared her throat, and again. "Perhaps I haven't been the best mother," she said after a moment. "But I tried. I did. I realize now it wasn't enough. You were always so emotional, so needy—"

"Not again." Emmeline closed her eyes at the familiar refrain.

"Hear me out. I don't express things well, Emmeline. I'm not good with words like you are. I'm not comfortable sharing my feelings. I never have been. But that doesn't mean I don't… love…you."

"Hard word for you to say, isn't it?"

"Yes."

"I've never heard you say *love* before." Emmeline locked her knees, lifted her chin. Today she would not fall apart. She would not leave in pieces. "You've never once told me you loved me."

"Because it wasn't necessary. I was your mother. You were my daughter—"

"And children like tenderness. They like affection. I craved it, Mother. Morning, noon and night."

"I know. You have such strong emotions, you feel everything so intensely. Just like your mother." Her voice quavered. "Everybody loved your mother. Her death devastated your grandparents. It broke William's heart, too, because he was Jacqueline's big brother. He adored her. That's why he wanted you."

"And you didn't."

"No, Emmie, I did. I wanted you and I tried my best with you, but you were inconsolable as an infant. You cried for the first six months of your life, day and night. Your grandmother was always reaching for you, wanting to comfort you, and I'd tell her no, that you were my daughter and I wanted to hold you. And I did. I used to walk with you in the nursery, back and forth, for hours. William would come up at two in the morning and he'd see me with you, and he'd tell me to come to bed. But I wouldn't. I was so determined to be a good mother. I was so determined to find a way to make you love me." She broke off, tears filling her eyes. "You never did."

"But I have always loved you. As a child I wanted nothing more than your approval. But you couldn't give me that."

"You were just so like her."

"Like Jacqueline."

Claire nodded.

"And you resented me for that," Emmeline concluded.

"I think I did."

"Why?"

"Because I wanted you to be like me."

Seated in the limousine next to Makin, Emmeline stared out the window, overwhelmed. So much had happened in just a handful of days. Alejandro's death. The revelation that Princess Jacqueline was the birth mother she'd never known. Her marriage to Makin. And then the scene with Claire in her bedroom. It was a lot to take in.

"Are you all right?" Makin asked, his voice a deep rumble in the darkness of the car.

"Yes," she answered faintly, her face averted, her gaze fixed on a point far away. Her heart felt battered. Bruised.

"Did something happen when you went upstairs after the ceremony?"

"How do you know?"

"I can see the change in you. I hear it in your voice."

It amazed her that he could already read her so well. "My mother came to see me."

"What did she have to say?"

Emmeline felt a hot rush of emotion and she closed her eyes so he wouldn't see. "She wanted me to know that despite appearances, she loved me. And I told her that I'd always loved her."

He was silent a moment. "But it wasn't exactly warm and satisfying?"

"No." She laughed, a quick, sharp laugh even as she blinked back tears. "But then, nothing with my mother ever is."

On board the plane, Emmeline curled into her chair and gave in to sleep.

While she slept, Makin called his close friend, Sultan Malek Nuri, to see how the Raha conference was going. Malek relayed that everything was going well, but, of course, everyone wished Makin was there.

"When do you return?" Malek asked. "I'd thought it was today, but maybe it's later tonight?"

"No. I'm actually en route to Marquette."

"Your Caribbean island?"

"Yes." Makin hesitated, wondering how to share his news, as Malek's wife Nicolette and her sisters were quite friendly, as well as distantly related, to Emmeline. Malek and Nicolette were also aware that Makin had never been a fan of Emmeline's. "I just got married," he said, believing the best way through something was directly.

"You...what?"

"I married Emmeline d'Arcy."

Malek Nuri was successful because he knew when to speak and when to hold his peace. But he did neither now. He laughed, a great rich laugh of pure amusement. "Makin, my friend, I thought you were just seeing her safely home."

"I was."

"What happened?"

"I couldn't let her go."

* * *

Emmeline didn't wake until they were in their final approach and close to landing.

"Where are we?" Emmeline asked, looking out the window. She'd expected a sea of sand, but instead it was blue underneath. Water.

"The Caribbean. We'll be landing on my island Marquette in the next few minutes, but look out the window, we're about to be treated to an incredible sunset now."

He was right. The sun was low in the sky, a great red ball of fire moments away from dropping into the ocean. The horizon was already turning orange and purple and Emmeline felt a thrill of pleasure. "It's gorgeous," she said.

"Dramatic, isn't it?"

She smiled, amused by his word choice. "So sometimes dramatic is good?"

His gaze met hers and held. "Yes. Sometimes dramatic is perfect."

On the ground a driver in a white open Jeep met them at the airstrip and drove them across the estate to a sprawling plantation house. The two-hundred-and-fifty-year-old house had been built in the colonial style, with a steep thatched roof, high ceilings and thick stone walls to keep the interior cool.

On entering the house, Emmeline discovered she could see the ocean from virtually every room, with the last lingering rays of light turning the sea into a parfait of purple, lavender and red.

The house itself was furnished in the dark woods of the colonial style, with a mix of Spanish, French and English antiques, furniture brought over from Europe during the sixteenth and seventeenth centuries. The fabrics, though, were all soft and light—white linens, red, green and blue cheerful tropical cotton prints.

It was a happy house, she thought, following Makin on the tour that ended in the spacious master bedroom with windows everywhere.

By the time they finished the tour, her luggage had already been brought in and a maid had unpacked her clothes into the large mahogany dresser and closet.

Makin left her so she could bathe and change for dinner. With
the door closed, Emmeline did a little twirl, her nerves almost
getting the best of her.

So this was it. No more solo rooms. They were married.
They'd share the master bedroom from now on.

She battled her panic by walking slowly around the bedroom,
trying to get comfortable even as her gaze avoided the bed. It
looked as though it was custom made, with a massive king-size
frame, and it was draped with sheer white linens. She knew that
it was in this bed that Makin would want to consummate the
marriage tonight—

She broke off, shook her head, unable to finish the thought.

Take it one step at a time, she told herself. *Bathe, dress, meet
Makin for dinner, and then worry about the rest later.*

It was a good plan, she thought thirty minutes later, but it
wasn't going to work.

She couldn't do this. Couldn't meet him for dinner and then
go to bed with him as if it was the normal thing to do. She barely
knew him. Had kissed him a few times, but that wasn't a relationship.

She was still panicking when the maid knocked on the door
and asked if Her Highness needed assistance. The maid, like the
rest of the staff, spoke French.

"Yes," Emmeline answered. "Can you please let Sheikh
Al-Koury know I'm not feeling well and won't be able to join
him?"

"You won't be joining him for dinner, Your Highness?"

"That's correct. Please tell him I don't feel well and I'm going
to bed."

CHAPTER FOURTEEN

HE didn't even knock. He just barged through the bedroom and into the bath where she was still chin-deep in now-tepid water.

"What's wrong?" he demanded, his gaze sweeping from the top of her head, where her blond hair was piled high in a knot, to the tips of her toes peeping from the water at the foot of the tub. "What's happened? Do you need to see a doctor?"

"No."

"You're not well?"

"No."

"Are you cramping? Are you queasy?"

"No!" She swallowed guiltily and slid a little deeper into the hot water. "I'm just...tired."

"Tired?"

"Yes. And I think I should just go to bed...you know...right now instead of after dinner."

"So you're not sick?"

"No. Not sick."

He swore beneath his breath and pushed a hand through his black hair, ruffling it on end. "So you're perfectly fine?"

"Other than feeling tired, yes."

He straightened, jaw tightening as his hands fisted at his side. "Do you have any idea how scared I was for you? I thought you were in pain. I thought you were miscarrying—"

"I'm not. And nothing's wrong. Okay? I was just..." She shook her head, looked away before glancing back at him. "Avoiding you."

"That's what this is all about?"

"Yes. I was nervous about consummating the marriage so I decided to stay in the bath and hide. Feel better?"

"No."

Now she felt foolish, embarrassed and angry with herself. Why did she think she could be the hero in a story if she wasn't even brave enough to face her husband? "I'm a coward, Makin. You know that. I'm shriveling to nothing in this cold bath because I'm hiding from you. Does that make you feel better?"

"No. But this will." And he leaned over the tub and scooped Emmeline from the bath, carried her soaking wet into the bedroom where he dropped her on the bed.

Before she could scramble backward, Makin moved over her, catching her wrists in his hands, pressing them down onto the bed, and straddled her hips with his thighs. "Stop hiding," he gritted through clenched teeth. "Stop running away and start living."

"Get off!" she choked, furious.

"I will when I feel like it," he answered, his gaze slowly sweeping over her wet puckered breasts. "Because isn't that what you do? You leave me outside, sitting by myself, waiting for my bride to join me when my bride in reality has no intention of joining me."

"I wanted to."

"If you wanted to, you would have come. Instead you send a maid to tell me you're going to bed."

"I was afraid!" she cried, trying desperately hard to twist free.

"Of what?"

"Of you. Of this." She was panting from exertion and frustration.

"And what's so scary about this?"

"All of it. Being naked. Being touched. Being known."

"Get over it. Because I'm going to touch you and know you and make you feel good if it's the last thing I do."

The heat in his eyes made her heart lurch. Emmeline drew a panicked breath which only emphasized the rise and fall of her bare, gleaming breasts. "Even if I say I don't want to?"

"You knew when we got married it would be a real marriage, and it's going to be." His gaze wandered slowly down her body, from the thrust of her collarbone to the peaked swell of her breasts, down her ribs to her small waist and rounded hips. "You have the most beautiful body, Emmeline. I can't wait to touch you and taste you, everywhere."

"I can," she huffed.

He had the gall to laugh as he lowered his head to kiss her collarbone. His mouth brushed across the length of the fragile bone and goose bumps covered her skin, making her nipples pebble tighter. "At least your nerve endings there work," he murmured, his mouth working its way down her collarbone to the upper slope of her breast.

Heat washed through her as his lips closed around one peaked breast, his mouth wet and warm against the cool hard nipple. She shuddered as he sucked, tension coiling deep inside her, making her aware there were things she didn't know, had never felt.

He moved to the other breast, laved the other nipple with attention even as his hands stroked her flat stomach and the curve of her hips.

He knew exactly how to make her feel. And she was feeling so much.

He was sucking harder on the nipple, and Emmeline pressed against him for relief, but it was impossible to find when his mouth was driving her wild. The pressure, tight and rhythmic, made her aware of how empty she felt, how much she needed him.

And she did need him. She needed him to touch her, kiss her, lick her, fill her. She'd let him do anything if he'd satisfy the aching emptiness within her. She'd never felt so tight and so hollow at the same time. Her body throbbed with the worst of the need between her legs.

His hand trailed down her flat belly, caressing her abdomen, skimming her belly button before stroking lightly across one jutting hipbone. She hissed a breath as his palm circled over the hipbone, sending sparks of sensation shooting through her. Her inner muscles squeezed, gripping nothing and yet she'd never felt so hot or wet before. She could feel the dampness of her own body, the hint of moisture at her thighs.

His fingers brushed over the hipbone again and then down her outer thigh and back up. Again and again he traced her thigh as his mouth followed the path his hand had just taken, tongue on her belly, circling her belly button and then outlining the curve of hipbone.

"Open your legs," he said, kissing the hollow where her thigh joined her pelvis. It was such a light kiss and yet she shuddered.

"Can't," she gritted and shuddered yet again as he kissed her through the golden curls at the juncture of her thighs. His warm breath made her go hot and then cold and little spots danced and exploded against her mind's eye.

"Why not?" he asked, sliding one finger down the front of her, through the curls and between her lips to touch her.

Emmeline gasped, eyes opening wide, and tried to scoot away. "I'll lose control."

"That's what you're supposed to do."

"No. Not good. Not good at all."

She heard him smother a laugh. "Why not?" he asked, stroking her again, his finger sliding up, then down once more, sliding deeper this time, over the tight bud to her slick inner folds.

"I'll feel too much," she gasped, thinking she was already feeling way, way too much. "And fall apart and that's never, ever good."

"But if you don't fall apart, you don't experience pleasure. And pleasure is a good thing."

He was still stroking her, and she was finding it harder and harder to focus on anything but the delicious sensations he was creating with his touch. But the pleasure wasn't just sexual, her entire body felt sensitive, intense and alive.

This time she didn't resist as he parted her legs and shifted his body to settle between her thighs.

She knew where he was, but it was still a shock when his mouth covered her sex, his lips and tongue touching, tasting her.

"Makin," she choked.

His tongue and fingers together caressed her, and the sensation seemed to grow, building, teetering between pleasure and pain.

Her hips rose as the tension coiled in her belly, tight and hard and far from soothing. His tongue stroked her, his fingers teased her, one filling her, sliding in and out and matching the flick of his tongue.

"Dammit," she choked, her body so hot, her skin growing damp. She wanted something else, wanted release but didn't know how to get it, find it, not when the pressure kept building until she felt mad with it.

"Can't, can't, can't," she repeated wildly, and just then he sucked on her sex, drawing tight on her until she arched and screamed, everything within her shattering, her body convulsing against his mouth, around his finger.

For long moments she struggled to catch her breath as her body jumped and jerked, exquisitely sensitive from head to toe. She'd never felt anything like that in her entire life. "That's an orgasm," she said, dazed.

She felt Makin smile as he kissed the inside of her trembling thigh. "Yes. That's an orgasm."

She drew a rough breath. "I can see why that could be addictive."

"See? You do need me," he said and the husky tone of his voice sent another wave of sharp pleasure racing through her.

"Maybe," she said sleepily.

"Just maybe?" he repeated, sitting up to look down at her.

With a jolt she realized he was still dressed. The sense of pleasure dimmed, overshadowed by a feeling of impropriety. Good girls didn't lose control…good girls didn't enjoy sex… good girls—

"Don't do it," he said curtly, interrupting the punitive voice within her, the one constantly taking her to task.

"Do what?" she asked.

"Ruin this by overthinking things."

"According to you, not thinking got me into trouble in the first place."

"Yes. But I'm not trouble. I'm your husband, and what we do together is a good thing, and you felt good until you started letting fear take over." He was unbuttoning his shirt, and then peeling it back from his powerful shoulders. His chest was all bronze muscle, his stomach so hard it looked as if it'd been carved from stone. "I don't subscribe to fear."

Her eyes grew round as his feet hit the ground and he stood next to the bed, unbuckling his belt and unzipping his pants, stripping his remaining clothes off one by one.

Alejandro had been naked with her that one night in March, but she hadn't really looked at him. Everything that night had been a haze of panic and fear, but Emmeline found it impossible not to look at Makin.

He was all male, incredibly male, from the wide shoulders to the tapered waist to the corded muscles of his thighs, and that didn't even include his very big, very erect member.

Her gaze locked on the length of his erection and it was a little too impressive. But then, everything about him was big.

Intimidating.

"That," she said, gulping, "will not fit in me."

His lips curved but his eyes burned with heat. "It will. Your body is an amazing thing."

"It's too big."

"You're very wet."

She cringed, shoulders rising to her ears. "It hurt with…him."

"You were a virgin, and it didn't sound as if he was gentle."

"And you will be?"

He stretched out on the bed next to her, his weight resting on his elbow. "Have I ever hurt you?"

His eyes were holding hers, his gaze intensely warm.

"No," she whispered.

"Nor would I. Ever."

Emmeline couldn't breathe, overwhelmed by emotion. He was so strong and sure of himself and she wanted to be that strong for him. "Promise?"

"Yes."

He lowered his head, covering her mouth with his. The kiss was extraordinarily slow, almost languid, as he took his time exploring the shape of her lips, the softness inside her mouth, knowing just how to turn her on again and make her feel.

Pretty soon her breath was catching in her throat, and her toes were curling with pleasure and her still-warm body grew hot.

He kissed her until she was reaching for him, her arm linking around his neck, needing to draw him even closer to her.

She loved it when he shifted and moved over her, welcoming his warmth and the weight of him. He was so big and hard and it felt right against her softness. She practically purred as his chest crushed her breasts, the hard planes of muscle rubbing across her tight nipples.

She was the one who parted her thighs, allowing him to sink between her hips, and then twisted her hips to slide the tip of his erection from her belly to between her legs. She exhaled hard when his shaft's large silken tip pressed against her wetness, the tip brushing across nerves that still felt sensitive from before.

It would be so easy to come again, she thought, as Makin kissed her deeply. His tongue probed her mouth, sliding across her lips and tongue even as his shaft slid across her slick opening.

She whimpered as he rubbed the tip up and down her once more. "Anything hurt?" he asked, looking into her eyes.

His eyes were so cool and yet hot, silver flecked with glowing gold. He was hard and fierce and focused and determined, everything she wasn't.

Her chest suddenly felt unbearably tight, and the backs of her eyes stung. If she weren't so afraid, she could love him. If she weren't so afraid of being left, rejected, broken, she could give herself to him.

But she was afraid. "No," she whispered, heart aching.

"I want you," he said.

Her arm tightened around his neck, her heart twisting, contorting, emotions on fire. "Take me."

Makin did, slowly filling her, groaning a little at the tightness of her hot sheath. She was almost too tight, and he feared hurting her. He paused, focused on her mouth and kissing her, and making her feel good. He could feel her grow hotter, wetter, and she was adjusting to his size. He pushed in deeper, still hanging on to his control. This time she wiggled beneath him, taking more of him. Makin groaned deep in his throat.

Once he was buried all the way in her, he rocked his hips,
oving forward just enough to press against her.

She gasped and he knew that hitch in her voice. Makin pushed
er long tumble of hair back from her neck, kissed her neck and
owly withdrew before plunging back in.

She gasped again. Blood surged within him, making his skin
ngle and his erection grow even harder.

He kissed her neck and the pink tips of her breasts as he
owly thrust in and out of her tight, hot body. He could hear her
reathe and see the color storm her cheeks and the deep flush
iffuse her breasts.

Makin used her breathing to tell him where she was and what
ie needed. It was easy to delay his pleasure. He'd learned con-
ol years ago but she was something new and gorgeous, and he
anted to make her feel good again, wanted to see her come this
me, and when she began to breathe in little pants he knew she
as close to shattering.

His fingers moved between their bodies as he increased the
mpo, his hips driving harder and deeper into her body, only to
ithdraw and drive deep again. He touched her, lightly circling
e small delicate nub with the pad of his finger. He felt her grow
ill beneath him, tensing, and he knew she was right there, ready.
e touched her again even as he thrust deep and she screamed.

This time he didn't let up. He kept thrusting in and out and she
rithed beneath him, her inner muscles clenching him, squeezing
m, wrenching his control away so that he couldn't hold back
iy longer. Makin felt as if he exploded, his body violently re-
asing into hers, and then shuddering with aftershocks.

It was the most intense orgasm he could remember. His entire
ody throbbed. But it wasn't just physical. His chest ached, too.

Makin kissed her, savoring the softness of her mouth and the
ay her lips parted beneath his. She tasted warm and sweet. She
sted like his.

Sensation ripped through him, centered in his chest. For a mo-
ent he couldn't catch his breath. It was a pain unlike any he'd
lt in years…a pain he'd only experienced twice before. When
s father died. And then his mother. It was pain created by love.

Makin lifted his head, gazed down into Emmeline's blue ey
and he finally understood why he'd claimed her. Why he'd i
sisted on marrying her and taking her away from her parents.

He loved her.

He needed her.

He wanted her.

Why hadn't he seen it before? Why hadn't he understoo
what he was feeling?

"Makin?" she whispered.

He stroked her hair, realizing now his desire to protect her.
make her his. It was because she *was* his. She'd been made f
him and he was here, born, created, for her. "Everything's good
he said, and he meant it. Everything was truly good.

Emmeline lay in the huge four-poster bed with the cool cott
sheet pulled to her chest, listening to Makin breathe.

He'd been asleep for an hour now, but she couldn't rela
couldn't sleep.

She liked him too much. Far too much. And that scared he

She'd married him to provide legitimacy for her baby, and y
here she was, falling for him. And falling for him was wron
It was dangerous.

She wanted to be brave and fearless. Wanted to wield a swo
and fight dragons, but the only dragons in her life were the dra
ons and demons inside of her. And those were still too big f
her to vanquish.

Twenty-five years of fear and insecurity didn't disappear in
week. Twenty-five years of needing acceptance didn't end aft
a night of sex.

The bad thing about fear was that it created more fear. An
she was afraid now.

Afraid of opening herself up and being crushed. Afraid to fe
and love only to discover more pain.

She couldn't do more pain. Not yet.

And so the only way to protect her heart was to guard it, an
yet around Makin she had so little control. Around him she fe
emotional and terrifyingly vulnerable.

Was this love? Could love be so full of fear?

She turned onto her side to look at him. The wooden shutters were partially open and moonlight fell across the bed in strips. A finger of light illuminated Makin's mouth. It was a firm, generous mouth that knew how to kiss her senseless, make her weak in the knees.

Gently she reached out to touch his cheek, a light touch, the briefest caress, as she didn't want to wake him. He needed his sleep.

He was a good man.

Better than she deserved.

CHAPTER FIFTEEN

EVEN though she'd been awake half the night, Emmeline woke a six and quietly slipped from bed to go dress in the spacious walk in closet. She changed into a long cotton skirt and a knit top an then grabbed her sandals and headed outside for an early walk

Skirting the island villa's immense and gorgeous gardens, sh descended the different terraces to walk the length of the cove on the beach of soft, powdery, pale sand.

Her head ached from lack of sleep. Her heart felt even wors

Makin heard her leave the bed and watched as she tiptoe from their room with sandals in her hand. He knew she hadn slept well, knew she'd been waiting impatiently for dawn so sh could escape.

After she left, he rose and showered and headed toward th kitchen for coffee.

Cook was already in there, baking. She greeted Makin effu sively and poured him a cup of steaming-hot coffee while ask ing where he and the queen would like to have breakfast. Th edge of his mouth lifted as he imagined Emmeline's reaction t being called his queen. "Outside," he said, still smiling faintl "on the upper terrace. Her Highness is out for a walk, so I'll wa to eat until she's returned."

He carried his coffee outside and leaned against the balus trade. He was still savoring his drink when Emmeline appeare on the lower terrace, cheeks pink, golden hair tousled. She looke young and fresh in her ruffled coral cotton skirt and white kn top, unbelievably appealing.

"You went to the beach?" he asked as she climbed the stone stairs to join him on the upper terrace.

"Yes. Looking for shells."

"Did you find any?"

She turned her hand over and showed him the three delicate shells in her palm. "These."

"Pretty," he said, admiring them before glancing up at her. "But do be careful. The old staircase at the lower terrace worries me. It should have been replaced years ago."

"I'll be careful."

"Did you sleep well?" he asked.

"I did. And you?"

So she wouldn't tell him the truth. She didn't trust him. Was determined to hide. "I was worried about you."

She looked down at the shells in her hand. "Why?"

"Because I care about you."

"Then don't worry. I'm great." She smiled then, a quick tight smile that didn't reach her eyes. "Have you eaten yet? I'm starving!"

After breakfast they spent the day snorkeling, sunbathing and swimming, both in the ocean and the big pool, and then midafternoon, after a long, leisurely lunch, Makin excused himself to take care of some business while Emmeline took a much-needed nap.

She woke up slowly, stretching lazily, her gaze fixed on the bright blue sky and turquoise water outside the bedroom window.

She'd slept well, and must have dreamed something lovely because she felt good, better than she had in days.

She liked Marquette. Could get used to coming here. And she'd enjoyed spending the day with Makin today. Earlier, as they swam and snorkeled and splashed in the pool, she'd laughed easily and felt happy. The real kind of happiness. But that kind of happiness scared her. It made you vulnerable, made you hurt when it ended.

Leaving bed, Emmeline disappeared into their ensuite bath to shower and wash her hair, taking time to blow it dry. With her towel wrapped around her toga-style, she headed back to the bedroom to figure out what she'd wear for that evening.

Makin was stretched out on the bed now, hands behind his head, a hot, hungry light in his eyes. "I almost joined you in the shower."

She blushed and tugged her towel tighter. "I shower alone," she said primly.

"Not for long."

Cheeks rosy, she disappeared into the closet.

"Cook has re-created our wedding dinner for us," Makin called to her.

"That's nice of her," she answered, emerging with a long ivory satin gown pieced together by long ropes of pearls. The dress had such a daringly low back and delicate beaded straps that Emmeline immediately thought of a harem girl. "What is this?" she asked, giving the hanger a shake.

"One of the dresses I ordered for you."

"When?"

"Yesterday when we were flying from Brabant. You were asleep and I was bored so I did a little online shopping."

She turned the dress toward her, inspecting the delicate label which she knew had been hand-sewn into the dress as the last step. "It's couture. This isn't something you buy online."

"I emailed the designer and requested a couple of dresses for the honeymoon."

"And how did you get it here so fast?"

"Had a plane go get it."

"Just like that?"

He shrugged. "I thought you'd look good in it."

"That's a ridiculous amount of money."

"I have a ridiculous amount of money."

She shook her head, lips pursing as she struggled not to smile. "You're shameless."

"I know. But you like my confidence." He left the bed and approached her, his gaze slowly examining her, starting at the top of her head and working his way down, possession darkening is eyes. "Maybe we should skip dinner tonight again," he said, drawing her into his arms, dipping his head to nuzzle her neck.

Her lips parted in a silent gasp as his mouth found nerves behind her ear, then along the column of her neck before kissing the hollow at her throat. "But Cook has re-created our wedding dinner," she protested hoarsely.

He found her lips, kissed her slowly, thoroughly, until she was clinging to him, her hands fisted in his shirt.

He lifted his head, gazed down into her eyes, and Emmeline blinked up at him, dazed. "Maybe we don't need dinner," she said breathlessly.

He smiled but there was a dangerous light in his eyes. "I don't, but you do. You're not eating enough, and you're eating for two." He gently but firmly set her back. "So I'll go shower and dress in the other room, but I will have you tonight, Emmeline. So do what you have to now, because later you'll be mine."

Pulse unsteady, Emmeline rang for a maid as she needed help fastening the tiny hooks of the seductive gown.

Finally dressed, Emmeline brushed her hair again, leaving it loose, and then did her makeup, focusing on her pale pink lips and dark smoky eyes. Finished, she rose from the dressing table, stepped back and glanced at herself in the mirror. As she turned, the long ropes of pearls swayed, brushing against her bare back, and the thin satin fabric strained to contain her breasts, while it kissed her belly and slid over her thighs. It was such a daring gown. It hinted at passion and seduction and very hot sex.

Sex. That's what they had together, wasn't it?

Hot sex, good sex, and she'd have to learn to be happy with that. Not to want more.

House staff bowed to Emmeline as she walked through the villa and directed her to the garden. In the garden more staff pointed her to the terrace below, the middle terrace, where a white silk tent had been erected on the lawn overlooking the sea, with torches at each of the tent's four corners, the long bamboo poles buried deep in the ground. Emmeline's pulse matched the torches tonight, her heart jumping and twisting like the gold flames.

As she climbed down the upper staircase to the middle terrace, she spotted Makin inside the tent, his back to her, his face toward the sea. He was wearing a white linen shirt and oatmeal linen slacks and she didn't think he'd ever looked quite so regal

"Do you ever wear traditional robes?" she asked him as she crossed the lawn and entered the tent where a table had been set for two. The tablecloth, a stunning watery blue silk, was the same clear blue of the ocean. A vase of white orchids and plumeria was in the center of the table while low white votive candles were nestled among the crystal and sterling silver.

"I do for business in Kadar. Sometimes at home. Why? Would you like me to wear the *thawb* and *keffiyeh* my countrymen do?"

"I don't know," she answered. "Maybe. Might help me to remember you really are Sheikh Al-Koury."

"Instead of…?" he prompted curiously.

"You." She swallowed hard, butterflies flitting wildly inside her tummy.

"And what am I?"

"Gorgeous."

He looked unaccountably pleased. "Am I?"

"You know you are!" she exclaimed, turning away, embarrassed to have even said that much.

Her gaze fell on the sitting area created in front of the table. A low couch was upholstered in the same matching blue silk as the tablecloth, with throw pillows in white. More white candles glowed in glass hurricanes on the ground. Emmeline could smell something tantalizing in the air and didn't know if it was his fragrance or the plumeria or a combination of the two.

"This is so beautiful and romantic," Emmeline said, suddenly overwhelmed by the need to be in Makin's arms, close to his chest. In his arms she felt good. Safe. In his arms she could almost believe he loved her…could almost believe that sex would be enough….

"My staff is very happy for us," he answered, filling a slender flute with icy-cold sparkling water for her, and then another for him.

"Just because I can't drink, doesn't mean you can't."

He shrugged, powerful shoulders rolling. "I don't need to drink to be with you. In fact, I prefer not to drink."

"Why?"

"I enjoy you too much."

She blushed, and took a seat on the low couch, her body suddenly sensitive and tingling everywhere.

She could feel Makin's gaze rest on her and it just made her heart race faster. He still overwhelmed her, but now it was in a sexy, wicked sort of way. She'd never felt beautiful with anyone but Makin before, had never felt so important before. In his eyes, she mattered.

Her heart turned over and hot emotion washed through her and suddenly Emmeline wasn't sure she could live without him.

She needed him. Wanted him. And yet love wasn't a sure thing.

Emmeline went hot and cold and her fingers tightened on the stem of the flute.

"Are you all right?" he asked, concern deepening his voice.

She nodded. "Yes." She forced herself to smile, the warm breeze caressing her, making her think of his hands on her skin. "Just a little overwhelmed...but in a good way."

"I hope so. I like having you here for me. It feels right. Makes the island feel like home."

Her heart ached all over again. She blinked back tears. "I love being here, too."

"You enjoyed today?"

"Very much."

"What did you enjoy most?"

She thought for a moment. "Swimming...snorkeling. The coral reef was amazing. So many beautiful fish."

"My mother loved it here, too. She believed it was very healing."

"Marquette was her island then?"

"My father bought it for her as a wedding gift. Growing up we spent many holidays here, but I haven't been to Marquette in years."

"Why not?"

"I'm not a boy anymore. I have work. Am usually too busy for pleasure trips."

She frowned a little at his intense work ethic. He was so driven, so ambitious. "Even men need to relax."

"My mother used to say the same thing to my father."

"And did he listen to her?"

"Most of the time."

"Good. So you have to listen to me, too."

Makin smiled at her, amused.

He'd told Malek Nuri that he'd married Emmeline because he couldn't let her go—which was true—but now looking at her in her daring pearl-and-satin gown, he knew it was more that that. He'd married her because she was made for him, destined for him, fated.

In Kadar her tears had moved him, but her laughter was twice as powerful. When she smiled at him he felt invincible. For her, he thought he could do anything.

And he would.

The evening passed slowly for Makin though. He didn't want to spend two hours at a table eating and talking, not when he found Emmeline and her satin-and-pearl gown so damn distracting. All evening the ropes of pearls and slinky satin fabric had teased, hugging her curves and revealing her smooth, flawless skin.

He was delighted when she passed on an after-dinner coffee. Back in their bedroom he shut the door, locking it and turned to discover Emmeline lifting her hair off her neck and presenting her back to him. "I'm going to need your help getting me out of this dress," she said.

Makin groaned under his breath. She looked like Aphrodite in that position, head slightly forward, hair piled in golden waves, arms up, her long slim back gorgeously exposed. And she was his.

Would always be his.

He hardened instantly, desire surging through him, making him feel even hotter and hungrier as his gaze swept over her, taking in the gleaming hair, the creamy nape, her bare back covered by just those long delicate strands. During dinner he'd been fascinated by the way the pearls draped across her skin, attached from the beaded shoulder straps of her gown to the dip in her spine where the ivory satin fabric just barely covered her bottom. Now he just wanted his hands on her bottom. Wanted to feel the softness of her skin on his.

And even though he was impatient to have her, he held himself in check, knowing she was still learning about sex and love. So he unhooked her gown carefully until the dress spilled to her feet in a tumble of silk and pearls.

The gown had been too bare for a bra. She stood now in just her high strappy heels and that tiny scrap of satin she called a thong.

Stifling another growl, he drew her backward and held her against him, his hands on her hips, her round pert butt pressed against his straining shaft.

God, he wanted to bury himself in her. Spread her thighs, drag her down on him and have her ride him.

But not yet.

His head dipped, he kissed the side of her neck, felt her shiver in response. He slid one hand from her hip up over the indentation of her waist, to her ribs to cup a bare breast. Her nipple was tight and hard against his palm and he rubbed it, teasing it, imagining it in his mouth, against the wet heat of his tongue.

She wiggled against him, her breast in his hand, the firm globes of her butt rubbing up and down along his erection and his control nearly snapped.

"Want you," he said thickly.

She turned in his arms, a tiny smile curving her lips, a bright glow in her eyes. For a moment he thought she looked happy, truly happy, and his heart turned over.

Makin caught her face in his hands, kissed her deeply, before stripping off his clothes. Naked, he sat down on the edge of the bed and pulled her onto his lap, lowering her slowly onto his hard shaft until she was settled firmly on his thighs, his erection embedded deeply inside of her.

With his hands on her hips he guided her, helping to set the rhythm he knew she liked. She was wet and slick and as he lifted her up and down on him, he felt her breathing quicken, heard her small quick gasps of pleasure. It was the sexiest sound and made him surge harder and deeper into her hot, wet body.

She came first and then he, and, spent, he dragged her backward on the bed to lie in his arms.

For long minutes they were quiet.

"Do you always do the right thing?" Emmeline asked, breaking the silence.

"I try," he answered, his voice deep, husky in the dark.

"Do you ever worry that doing the right thing might not always be the right thing?"

"No."

She turned restlessly in his arms, the sheets sticking to her damp skin, resenting him just a little for his confidence. How nice it must be never to doubt oneself! "But doing the right thing might not always be right," she persisted. "Doing the right thing might actually be the worst thing you can do."

"How so?" he asked, lazily, lifting her hair in his hand, letting it slide through his fingers.

Makin's ease with her made her almost crazy. He seemed so content, so calm and self-assured. It wasn't fair. She never felt calm and content. She almost always felt as if she were one step away from disaster.

"My uncle adopted me out of duty," she said, drawing a deep breath, "just as you have married me out of duty. I worry that you and my uncle have both made the same mistake. Your decisions weren't based on love, but doing the right thing, and I worry that later you might come to resent me the way Claire resented me. I think she wanted to be my mother but then felt burdened by the responsibility."

"I'm not William or Claire, so I can't answer for them, but I can answer for me. You will never be a burden. I chose to make you my wife. There was no gun to my head, no external pressure. It was a decision I freely made and, Emmeline, I'm a man of my word. I've made a commitment to you and the baby and you are now my family. Both of you."

"But someday you'll want children of your own," she said, "and I'm afraid you'll love them more—"

"No."

"You will." She rose up on her elbow to look down at him. "It's natural."

His hand wrapped around a fistful of hair and he gave it a gentle tug. "Emmeline, I won't ever have biological children. I can't."

"Why not?"

"My father's disease is genetic." After the slightest pause he continued, "I didn't get the disease itself, but I carry the genes. I can't take the risk of having children and giving them my father's disease. The disease ravished my father. The end was brutal. He suffered terribly."

"But you talked about starting a family…"

"And I will. There are so many children in this world that need parents, love, a stable home. I've always planned on adopting."

"Were you ever going to tell me?"

"I'm telling you now."

"Yes, but what if I married you hoping to have children with you?"

"But you didn't."

"What if I want more children?"

"I hope you do. As an only child, I always wanted brothers and sisters. I'd love to adopt down the road, give our little one siblings."

"And we would adopt those?"

"Yes."

"And you would love all of them, regardless of their parentage?"

"Yes."

"How can you be so sure?"

"Because they'd be ours, yours and my children."

She lay back down next to him, facing him, scooting as close to him as she could, wanting to absorb his warmth and strength. She wished she could tell him how much she loved his strength and his confidence. She wished she could let him know that he inspired her…made her want to be bolder, more courageous.

"You really will love my baby?" she whispered, face tipped up to his.

"Yes," he answered, smoothing her hair back from her face. "I will be a good father. I had a great father. He taught me what love is."

Emmeline's eyes felt heavy but she wouldn't let herself fall asleep. She wanted to look at Makin.

She didn't know how he'd done it, but she'd fallen for him, fallen hard and fast.

She loved him. But she didn't trust love. In fact, loving him made everything worse.

Because now he had the power to hurt her. Now he could break her heart.

And maybe he did want her, but Emmeline knew that sexual desire waned, and she feared that when the newness of their coupling wore off, he'd lose interest.

He'd go. If not physically, then emotionally. And that would drive her mad. She'd feel like desperate Emmeline again, the girl who couldn't ever get enough love. And Emmeline hated being needy. She'd hated that she wanted so much more than her parents could give. And the truth was, she already wanted more from Makin. Sex wasn't enough. She couldn't just be his woman in bed when he needed release. She wanted his heart.

Fighting tears, Emmeline leaned forward and gently touched her lips to his.

If only she were different.

If only she were someone stronger. Calmer, tougher, someone less brittle. Someone like Hannah. Maybe then she could trust. Maybe then she could believe there was something good about her, something someone could love.

But she wasn't Hannah. Regretfully, she wasn't anything like Hannah.

Emmeline's morning walk felt like a death march. She walked in circles on the beach, arms wrapped around her waist as she faced the truth.

She couldn't do this anymore. Couldn't remain in this paradise and swim and play and make love to Makin as if this was really a honeymoon.

This was no honeymoon. It was hell. She was living in hell and it was her fault.

She'd fallen in love with Makin. She wasn't supposed to fall in love. She was supposed to have been smart, strong, safe.

Instead, she loved him and needed him, and the depth of her emotions terrified her. They were too much.

If only she hadn't fallen in love with him then maybe she could have played the game…floated through a marriage of convenience with dignity and grace. But there was nothing dignified about what she was feeling.

She felt consumed by fear, consumed by need and pain. There was no way Makin could ever love someone like her…someone so fearful and broken…someone so damaged.

He'd soon discover just how much she needed him and it would overwhelm him. Her needs overwhelmed everyone.

Better to leave now while she could. There was no way she was strong enough for a prolonged goodbye. Better to do it quickly and cleanly, one hard cut today, a total break, and then move on.

Emmeline exhaled in a quick rush, knowing she was kidding herself. It wouldn't be a clean break. It'd be brutal, but she'd have to be brutal with Makin to make him leave.

She inhaled sharply, her heart hurting, burning, as she pictured him walking away.

He'd be okay, she told herself, shoving a hand across her mouth to stifle a cry. He'd be fine. He was tough. Strong. He'd survive without her. She was the one who might not make it without him.

Makin was standing on the upper terrace, staring out over the sea, when she returned from her morning walk.

He didn't look at her as she climbed the steps and Emmeline knew immediately something was wrong. He leaned against the wall, his gaze fixed on the ocean, the morning breeze ruffling his dark hair.

"Nice walk?" he asked casually.

"Yes."

"You're okay?" he persisted.

She tugged a wild tendril away from her eyes. "Yes. Why?"

"I thought I heard you crying while you were walking below."

A lump rose to her throat. She had been crying, but she didn't want him to know. "No."

"I could have sworn it was you."

The lump grew bigger. Emmeline's mouth quivered and she bit ruthlessly into her bottom lip. "It was the wind."

He finally looked at her. His gaze shuttered, expression cool. "I can still hear it in your voice."

She forced a smile, closed the distance between them and kissed his shoulder. He was so tall, so powerful, and completely addictive. "You're imagining things," she said lightly, knowing that soon she'd tell him it was over. Sometime in the next hour or two everything would change forever. "I'm going to go shower and dress. Have you had breakfast already?"

"No."

"Give me fifteen minutes and I'll be right back."

Emmeline headed for their bedroom aware that Makin watched her every step until she disappeared inside the house. He knew something was wrong. He'd press her for the truth this next time, and she would tell him.

It happened just the way she'd expected. They were still at breakfast, lingering over coffee, talking about what they wanted to do that day when Makin abruptly told her he knew she was upset, that he'd been awakened last night by the sound of her crying.

"Don't tell me nothing is wrong," he said flatly. "Obviously something is. What?"

He didn't skirt problems but ran directly at them, head-first. Emmeline felt a rush of intense love and admiration. He really was good, strong. He needed someone at his side who was as good and strong.

She was neither.

Nor would she ever be.

"I changed my mind," she said quietly, toying with the handle on her cup. "I changed my mind," she repeated, louder, more firmly. "I can't do this after all."

"Do what?" he asked, almost too gently.

She steeled herself against regrets, wouldn't tolerate second thoughts. "Do...this...be here with you like this, as if I'm really your wife."

"You *are* my wife."

She forced herself to meet his eyes, hold his gaze. "I'm not, not truly."

His shoulders squared. He seemed to grow even taller. "You said the vows. You have my ring on your finger."

Emmeline glanced down at the enormous stone weighting her finger. Her heart turned over. His mother's ring. Suddenly frantic to be free of all this emotion, fear and pain, she tugged the ring off her finger and held it out to him. "Take it, then. I won't wear it again."

"No."

"I can't do this. I thought I could. But I was wrong. It won't work. I'm not the right woman for you, I'm not a woman who can love you the way you want—"

"You don't know what I want."

"I do. You want a woman like your mother, you want a good woman, a loving woman, a woman who will make your life magical and special, who will love you no matter what...but I don't know how to love like that."

He studied her for an endless moment, his expression grave, gray eyes empty. "I don't believe you. I think you're just scared—"

"I don't love you, Makin." It killed her to say it. It was a lie, an absolute lie, but she knew she had to be brutal, knew she had to hurt him, and she did. She saw his expression change, his features harden because she knew then with absolute certainty that she did love him. But he couldn't know or he'd never let her go. She battled for composure. "I will never love you."

Again he looked at her, no emotion in his mouth or eyes. "Why not?"

If she was going to cut the ties that bind, if she was going to set him free—set them both free—she couldn't just go through the motions. She had to make the cut sharp and deep.

Brutal, she told herself, *be brutal and finish this.*

Her lips curved and she forced a mocking note into her voice. "Do you really need to ask?"

"Yes."

She shrugged carelessly even as her heart burned. "You'll never be Alejandro."

He didn't even blink. He made no sound. He just looked at her, intensely, searchingly, and she kept her smile fixed, her lips curving cruelly. "I loved him," she added. "You know I loved him—"

"You told me you never did."

Another indifferent shrug. "I know what I said, but it was a lie. An act. I was playing you the entire time."

Finally, a flicker of emotion in his silver eyes. "Why, Emmeline?"

The husky note in his voice was almost her undoing. She struggled to breathe when her throat was squeezing closed. She couldn't do this, couldn't be so hurtful and hateful. But if she didn't hurt him badly, he'd forgive her. He was that kind of man. So she had to be hideous. Terrible. Beyond redemption. She had to make sure he let her go.

Forever.

"Because sometimes we play games to get what we want."

"And what did you want?"

"A name for my baby. A story to give the press."

"And I'm that story?"

She nodded. "Even when we divorce, I will tell everyone you fathered my child. When the baby is born, I will give him or her your name. I can be a divorcée and have a good life. I just couldn't as an unwed pregnant princess."

"I could demand a paternity test, make the results public."

"You wouldn't."

"I would."

"You married me to do the right thing. You are a man who believes he can make a difference, and you do."

"But now you're done with me."

Her chest constricted, her heart was on fire. "Yes."

"You used me."

"Yes." She extended her hand, the ring balanced on her palm. "Take it. Give it to your next wife. Let's hope you make a better choice than you did with me."

Makin pushed away from the table without a word. Emmeline waited, feeling as if life as she knew it had come to an end.

There would never be another Makin Al-Koury. There would never be a man with his grace or strength or courage.

She sat for another fifteen minutes hoping against hope that he'd come back, grab her, shake her, kiss her, tell her she was a fool. Because she was a fool. A frightened fool.

But he didn't return.

Instead she heard the distant roar of an engine. Emmeline froze, cold all over. It was Makin's plane.

Makin was leaving her.

Emmeline rose, stood in place, her heart thudding heavily, hollowly in her ears.

What had she done? What had she done to him? To them?

She raced from the terrace to the upper garden, and the distant roar of the jet's engines grew stronger. Panic flooded her. What was the matter with her? What was she thinking? When would she stop being so afraid?

She had to stop him, had to catch him, had to let him know she was wrong. Emmeline dashed down the stone stairs of the terraces. The plane would be taking off any minute. There was no way to reach the runway in time but maybe she could catch the pilot's attention, maybe Makin would see her on the beach.

Emmeline tore down the narrow wooden stairs, taking the white painted steps two at a time, running across the sand to the water.

The engines grew louder. She spun around, waving her arms overhead as the white jet appeared directly over her. It rose swiftly into the sky. She ran deeper into the water, waving madly. Surely Makin would see. Or the pilot. *Someone.*

But the jet kept banking right, ascending steeply, soaring over the ocean, letting Marquette fall behind.

Emmeline's arms fell to her sides. For several minutes she just stood there as waves crashed and broke against her legs.

He'd gone. He'd gone just as she feared he would.

Because she'd chased him away.

CHAPTER SIXTEEN

EMMELINE stayed on the beach for an hour, and then another, unable to leave the cove. Her legs wouldn't hold her. She couldn't stop crying. She'd never hated herself so much in her entire life, and that was saying a lot because Emmeline was an expert in self-loathing.

But enough was enough.

When would she grow up? Become that strong prince with the sword who was slaying dragons instead of the princess in the tower?

When would she be someone she could admire? When would she stop acting out of fear?

She'd hurt Makin because she was afraid he'd hurt her. She'd gathered her love for him and turned it into a weapon, slashing out at Makin as if he was the dragon.

He was no dragon. He was a prince. A hero.

The man she adored with all her heart. Even though it was a broken and battered heart.

But hearts mended and love could heal and she could become stronger. She could become brave. She just had to tell Makin the truth.

That she loved him…more than she'd loved anyone…and she would work on changing if he would just be patient. If he'd just give her the chance.

And somehow, in her heart, she knew he would. Because he was that kind of man.

She wiped away tears with the back of her arm. She should

go back to the house. She'd been on the beach for hours but she needed to gather her composure. Even though Makin was gone, she couldn't be seen with a swollen, red face—princesses didn't cry in public—and so she lingered for another half hour on the beach, watching a storm move across the horizon, ominous clouds gathering in the sky.

The first raindrops fell as the wind blew in a gust that lashed at the palm trees. Emmeline cast a glance at the now-dark sky. The clouds were black. The wind began to howl. Brushing the sand off the back of her skirt, she quickly headed for the stairs.

The wind buffeted Emmeline as she climbed the old staircase, and for a moment she paused, feeling the stairs sway and creak. She shuddered a little as they swayed again. Suddenly there was a loud pop and crack and Emmeline grabbed the staircase rail as she felt the wooden stairs begin to collapse.

The baby, she thought in panic, as the wooden structure folded in on itself like a row of dominoes and she scrambled backward, leaping into the soft wet sand just as the entire staircase came crashing down.

Emmeline sat up and put a hand to her middle. She hadn't fallen hard. It hadn't been a very high jump. She hadn't even had the wind knocked out of her. The baby couldn't have been hurt.

But it was a wake-up call, she thought, stepping away from the wooden debris. She needed to be more careful.

Getting to her feet, she shouted for help. The wind was so loud she was sure it devoured her voice. She shouted again anyway. And again. No one came.

The rain slashed down and the wind tore at her hair and Emmeline sat on the wet beach with her arms wrapped tightly around her knees as she struggled to think of a way to get off the private beach.

She couldn't think of anything that might be safe. She'd have to ride the storm out.

Time slowed, blurred. Minutes became hours. Darkness was now rapidly descending, and the wind still howled, but Emmeline thought she heard an engine.

Had Makin returned? Had he heard she was missing and flown back to find her?

But no one could fly in this weather, and the intense winds would make it impossible to land safely on the small island airstrip.

Emmeline fought panic. The wind kept screaming, the tide kept rising, and the waves were breaking just feet away from her now. If the tide got much higher, she'd be swimming soon.

She suddenly stilled. Was someone shouting her name?

Could it be? Or was it more wishful thinking?

A light glowed overhead. Someone *was* up there. She rose unsteadily shouted for help.

The yellow light shifted. "Emmeline?"

Makin.

Her heart stopped. "Down here! Makin, I'm here!"

He moved the lantern, crouching on the edge of the terrace above her, at the place the staircase used to be. She couldn't see his face, the lantern too low, shining down on her, but she found his size and shape so very reassuring.

"What are you doing out here?" he shouted.

"I was trying to find you—"

"Have you lost your mind? It's a bloody hurricane!"

"It wasn't when you left."

"Stay right there. Don't move."

He reappeared in minutes, anchoring a long rope in one of the metal rings which had supported the stairs.

Emmeline squinted against the darkness, trying to see through the rain, as Makin took the rope, wrapped it around his waist and rappelled down the crumbly face of the cliff. He was like a pirate in one of those old movies, leaping from the rigging of one tall ship onto the rigging of another.

With the lantern flickering she could see that the rain had soaked his shirt, flattening the fabric, outlining his back and the corded muscles in his arms.

He continued his descent until he could reach her. "Give me your hand," he said, bracing his feet against the rock.

"Makin, you can't—"

"Don't! Don't ever tell me what I can and can't do. I know what I can do. Now give me your hand."

Biting her lip she put her hand into his. His fingers immediately closed around hers. "Hold tight," he commanded, as he slowly pulled her into the circle of his arms, his body sheltering hers as he adjusted his grip on the rope.

"Turn and face me," he said, his voice in her ear. "Wrap your legs around my waist—"

"Makin—"

"Not interested, Emmeline. Do as you're told. Slide up and wrap your legs around my waist. Lock your feet by your ankles. And hang on tight. Got it?"

She nodded against his chest and, heart pounding, she felt him begin the arduous climb back up the cliff.

The rain was pouring down and she could feel his heart thud against hers as he lifted them, hand over hand, up the rocky face.

Makin was breathing hard as they reached the top. With one foot on the top of the cliff, and the other still planted on the rocky face, he pushed Emmeline onto the flat terrace before pulling himself up and over to join her.

Emmeline stared at him wide-eyed as he dragged a hand through his hair and shoved it off his face. "You are in so much trouble," he gritted through clenched teeth. "You have no idea how angry I am. You could have been hurt. You could have hurt the baby—"

"I was trying to stop you."

"I was coming back."

"I didn't know." She was shivering now, chilled by her wet clothes as well as his furious expression. "And I'd said all those terrible things, Makin, said hateful things, and you were right to go—"

"I would never leave you."

"But you took off—"

"I had something to do."

"I didn't think you were coming back."

"You have so much to learn, but I'm not doing this now. Go to the house. Shower, dress, have a snack and then meet me in the living room in half an hour. You do not want to be late. Understand?"

Emmeline showered, dressed, sipped some hot sweet tea and nibbled on some buttered toast and was in the living room in twenty minutes, not thirty. Makin wasn't there. But someone else was.

A tall, lean man with graying blond hair and darkly tanned skin turned around when he heard the click of her heels. He was wearing jeans and cowboy boots and a Western-style belt with an enormous oval silver buckle.

"Oh, excuse me," Emmeline said, drawing up short. "I didn't realize we had a guest."

The man was as tall as Makin and just as broad through the shoulders. He had piercing blue eyes and a firm mouth above a hard, uncompromising chin. "My God," he muttered. "Jacqueline."

Goose bumps covered Emmeline's arm. "What did you just say?"

"Unbelievable," he said, taking a step toward her, his expression incredulous. "You look just like her."

He was an American, with a Texas drawl. A real cowboy? "Who?" she whispered.

"Your mother."

For a moment she couldn't breathe. "You knew her?"

"Yes."

"You know who I am?" she asked faintly.

"My other daughter."

Emmeline's legs buckled. She reached for a chair and sat down. "*Other* daughter?"

He nodded, brow furrowed, blue eyes darkening with emotion. "Hannah's twin."

"Hannah?" she choked.

"Hannah Smith. Your sister."

Hannah was her sister? Her twin? Impossible. Impossible. "How…what…?" Emmeline shook her head, unable to get the words out.

"Princess Jacqueline had twins." It was Makin who spoke.

He'd quietly entered the living room a few moments earlier and moved to Emmeline's side. "Two baby girls, and you were separated at birth. One baby went to Texas, and the other to your family in Brabant."

Emmeline leaned forward, covered her mouth as she stared across the room to the American. "I can't believe this…"

"I finally put it all together yesterday," Makin said, his hand on her back. "I called Jack to confirm my suspicions. Once I told him what I knew, he got on the first flight he could for St. Thomas, and I brought him here."

Emmeline couldn't look away from the blond, weathered Texan with his boots and jeans. "You're really my…father?"

Jack Smith nodded. "I had no idea there were two of you," he said gruffly. "I can't believe I didn't get to raise both of you. I should have."

Her eyes burned and she drew a quick breath. "What was she like? My mom?"

"Like you." Jack's voice deepened, roughened. "Smart. Kind. Funny. And the most beautiful thing I'd ever seen in my life."

Emmeline dashed away tears. "You loved her?"

"More than I can say."

The three of them had dinner and they talked nonstop, Emmeline asking questions and Jack answering them with Makin just listening.

Now and then during dinner Emmeline would have to brush away tears and she'd look at Makin and discover him watching her and the expression on his face…the look in his eyes…it nearly broke her heart.

He didn't just want her body. He didn't just want sex. He wanted her.

He cared for her.

He might even love her.

Blinking back tears she turned her attention to her father who was telling her how he'd met her mother. Jacqueline had been on a goodwill tour of North America and Jack, a Texas Ranger, had been assigned to her security detail while visiting Texas.

"We fell in love somewhere between Austin and San Antonio.

We made love just once. It was hurried and risky, but I loved her. I was crazy about her and had imagined appearing before her parents in Brabant and asking for her hand. But after she returned home, I never heard from Jacqueline again. I had no idea she was pregnant until one day a woman shows up on my ranch with an infant, tells me that Jacqueline has died and this is our daughter."

"And this woman never told you there had been another baby?" Emmeline asked, leaning forward.

He shook his head. "No. Not a word, and I can assure you, that if I had known about you, Emmeline, I would have come for you. And no one, not even the King and Queen of Brabant, could have kept me from you."

Emmeline glanced at Makin and then back to her father. "Does Hannah know about me? That I'm really her sister?"

Makin nodded. "She does now."

"I want to see her."

"She's on the way," Jack said. "She should be here in the morning."

Later, after everyone had gone to bed and the house was dark and quiet, Emmeline turned to face Makin. "You really do love me," she whispered. "I wasn't sure before. I thought it was just sex you wanted, or maybe a woman like Hannah—"

"Oh, no, I definitely don't want Hannah." He put a finger to her lips when she opened her mouth to protest. "She is brilliant and your twin sister, but I don't feel even a spark of attraction for her. Now you...I can't keep my hands off you."

Emmeline closed her eyes, lips parting as he kissed the side of her neck, her collarbone and lower, on her breast. "You'd better stop, Makin. I won't be able to talk pretty soon."

"Good. We've talked enough for tonight."

"But there are things I have to say—"

"You don't."

"I do. I need you to forgive me for saying hurtful things and pushing you away—"

"I already have." He tucked a long strand of hair behind her ear. "I love you."

"You should hate me for hurting you, for saying unkind things."

The edge of his mouth lifted. "I can't hate you. I could never hate you. You were scared. I know that."

"It's that easy? No grudges? No simmering anger? No lingering resentment?"

He laughed softly, pulling her onto his chest, and kissed her again. "No."

"Why not?"

"Because you're my wife—"

"Even if it's by default?"

He laughed again and kissed her slowly. "Not by default. This is fate, my darling. You were made for me."

"Even with all my flaws and faults?"

"You're not flawed. You're just you, and real, and perfect for me."

"I love you, Makin."

"I know."

"You do?"

He nodded, kissed her gently, and then again, this time deepening the kiss so that his tongue teased hers, tasting her. "Yes."

"How?"

"Because you can't contain your feelings—"

"I knew it!"

He laughed softly and kissed her again. "And that's a good thing, Emmeline. I need your warmth and your energy and your passion for life. I've spent these past fourteen years pouring myself into my work but I'm ready to have more...I want and need more. I want and need you."

"Why? Why me?"

"I have no idea, but no one has mattered to me here," he said, pausing to touch his chest, just over his heart, "until I entered Mynt and saw you there in that tight little turquoise dress. And I came alive. For you."

"You really, truly do love me!"

"I really, truly do. And we're good together. We're meant to be together."

"How can you be so sure? We've only been together a week."

"My father knew my mother just days before he married her. They had twenty wonderful years together."

She exhaled carefully, her heart so full it ached. "I would love to have twenty wonderful years with you."

"Not me. I want at least forty."

She had to blink back the hot rush of tears. "That does sound better."

"At least forty," he repeated. "We can watch our children grow, marry and have children. How does that sound?"

"Like the very best happily-ever-after ending I've ever heard!"

EPILOGUE

Seven months later

IT WAS a bright winter morning in Nadir, at the city's best hospital in the wing reserved for the Al-Koury royal family. It had been a long night for those in the labor and delivery room, though, and Emmeline had been grateful for her husband's and sister's support.

Nineteen hours of contractions had left Emmeline exhausted and the pain was just getting worse.

Gripping Hannah's hand tightly, Emmeline cried out as the latest contraction gripped her belly. The contractions were right on top of each other now with no rest time anymore. "Hurts," she choked, perspiration beading her brow, body trembling uncontrollably.

"You're almost there," the nurse said soothingly.

Emmeline shook her head. "Really hurts."

Makin glared at the nurse. "Give her something for the pain, now!"

"Too late," the nurse answered crisply, stepping around the sheikh and checking the monitor that tracked Emmeline's and the baby's heart rates. Both were doing just fine.

"What do you mean, too late?"

The nurse stepped around Makin again. "The baby is crowning. He or she is here."

But Makin was beside himself. "And where the hell is the doctor?"

"On his way. But your little one is impatient to see the world and has decided not to wait." The nurse gave Emmeline a calm, encouraging smile. "Your Highness, on the next contraction you are going to take a deep breath and push—"

"Without giving her something for the pain?" Makin demanded.

"No, Makin, she can't," Hannah snapped at him from the opposite side of the bed, exasperated by his bellowing and the only one in any condition to tell him to pull himself together. "You insisted on being in here," she added tartly, pointing to the door, "but you're not helping Emmeline when you roar like that. So help her, or go."

Makin's jaw hardened as he swallowed, but his expression softened the moment he glanced down at Emmeline. "I'm sorry," he apologized, smoothing her hair back from her damp face. "I hate seeing you in pain."

"I'm okay."

"Not okay," he corrected, leaning over to kiss her. "You're amazing."

"All right, Your Highness," the nurse said, watching the contractions build on another machine. "It's time to meet your little one. Take a deep breath and push. Give me everything you can."

With Hannah squeezing one hand, and Makin holding the other, Emmeline focused all her energy on bringing her baby safely into the world.

"That's it," the nurse exclaimed. "You did it. Your daughter is here."

And then the baby cried, a loud piercing cry.

"Oh, Emmie, she's gorgeous!" Hannah exclaimed, leaning over to kiss her sister's cheek. "Congratulations!"

A girl, a daughter, Emmeline silently repeated as she glanced from the nurse who held the squalling infant, to her husband, Makin, who only had eyes for the newborn.

"May I hold her?" he asked the nurse gruffly.

"Do you want to wait until I clean her up?"

"No. I've been waiting forever to meet my daughter."

Emmeline's eyes filled with tears as the nurse handed the slippery, shrieking baby to Makin. He held her close to his chest, his big arms cradling her securely, as if that's what his arms were made to do. "Jacqueline Yvette," he said softly, and the baby stopped kicking and crying.

"What do you think of the name?" he asked Emmeline, carrying the tiny infant around the foot of the bed and over to meet her mother for the first time.

Emmeline gazed down at her naked baby daughter nestled in Makin's powerful arms. She was a red-faced little thing with a thatch of dark hair and a big strong kick. "It's perfect," she said huskily.

Makin leaned over to kiss her. "Just like her mother."

Blinking back tears, Queen Hannah Jacqueline Patek quietly slipped out of the room to go tell her husband that the next generation of beautiful royal princesses had just been born.

* * * * *